Carnival Tale

for

Blind Ben See

CARNIVAL TALES FOR BLIND BEN SEE

ROGER L. ROBBENNOLT

FOREST OF PEACE
Publishing

Suppliers for the Spiritual Pilgrim
Leavenworth, KS

Other Books by the Author:
(available from the publisher)

Tales of Gletha the Goatlady
Tales of Hermit Uncle John
Tales of Tony Great Turtle

CARNIVAL TALES FOR BLIND BEN SEE

Library of Congress Cataloging-in-Publication Data

Robbennolt, Roger.
Carnival tales for blind ben see / Roger L. Robbennolt.
p. cm.
ISBN 0-939516-44-6
1. United States—Social life and customs—20th century—Fiction.
2. Carnivals—United States—Fiction. 3. Boys—United States—Fiction.
I. Title.
PS3568.02224C37 1999
813'.54—dc21 99-18179
CIP

published by
Forest of Peace Publishing, Inc.
PO Box 269
Leavenworth, KS 66048-0269 USA

printed by
Hall Commercial Printing
Topeka, KS 66608-0007

1st printing: March 1999

Dedication

To Hillis Slaymaker,
who inadvertently gave me life —
in more ways than he's ever known.

To Verlie Ward,
who challenged me to grow
as a spirit-filled man and a storyteller.

To the Carnival Folk,
who created a community
of light in the darkness.

And, as always, to Pat,
whose saving love story
provides the heart of the matter.

the heron

> *. . . a symbolism common to them all (wading birds) was that of good struggling with evil, and so later of Christ combating the Evil Spirit and his agents — no doubt because all these birds are formidable enemies of snakes and of a host of small animals and reptiles that are destructive or disagreeable . . . the Indians of North America say that herons contain the souls of wise men who have returned to the earth on mysterious pilgrimages . . . . The heron's preference for solitary places has also made of it one of Christian symbolism's rare living examples of silence, a silence which is precious because it leads the human being from reflection to wisdom.*
>
> — Louis Charbonneau, *The Bestiary of Christ*

> *Memories hurt. They are not completely healed while they still hurt.*
>
> — Madeleine L'Engle, *A Live Coal in the Sea*

Publisher's Note

As a footnote to the Author's Note on page 9, this book is aimed at mature youth and adults. It is not meant for anyone under the age of fourteen.

Table of Contents

PREFACE

A Washington State Penitentiary counselor had invited me to enable a session with twenty maximum-security prisoners. Like me, they had experienced catastrophic childhood abuse. I shared my journey through darkness into the mottled light of the present using as a vehicle some of the tales in this book.

Many of these "hardened criminals" wept. One whispered, "How come you could go through what you went through, and you're still out there and I'm in here?"

"Well," I responded, "there are three reasons. First, I keep a yellowing piece of paper in my shaving mirror. On it I've scrawled a line which I've needed to see at the start of every day: 'No situation need destroy you. Your response to the situation may destroy you.'

"Second, I'm real competitive. If I let the anger and self-loathing resulting from my mindsick daddy's abuse completely screw up my life, then he wins. I have to constantly fight the possibility of Daddy winning.

"But most important, I've always been surrounded by the people in my stories. Most of them were outcasts from respectable society. All of them were deeply scarred by one kind of terror or another. However, they proved that underneath the scarring, they were sacred — were people of fantastic worth.

"They would never let me have a pity party — never let me feel the world owed me anything just because I'd been through hell. Since they'd all been wounded, they reached out to a troubled kid and in the process released healing love. They saved me from destruction and despair. The memory of their hugs and words keeps me from lashing out at everything and everyone."

A man who seldom spoke raised his hand, "I think you've just been telling us who we really are, but I wish you'd stick to stories. You're beginning to sound a little preachy."

The men broke up.

Another shouted over the laughter, "Hey, Rog. I think yuh oughta' put all this stuff in a book for us: what yer daddy did to yuh when yuh was fourteen and how yuh ran away with the carnival and ended up fergivin' 'im."

I responded defensively, "I think there will be too many people who may be unwilling or afraid to wade through the darkness to get to the laughter and light."

"Aw, baloney! Yuh been tellin' us to risk tryin' new stuff. Yuh gotta' practice what yuh preach. Yuh gotta' risk sharin'. It'll help people understand what might be goin' on in the guy standin' next to 'em."

There were murmurs of assent.

I was obviously hesitant.

A man in the back stood up and threw down a final challenge: "You've said you really care about us. Well then, write the damn book. It might help us stay out when we get out — and keep some from gettin' in."

Dear prison brothers, you convinced me. Here's the book.

Author's Note

I have been asked why darkness descends in this book's second tale immediately on the heels of the first, which is light, funny and affirming. I'm writing faith exploration in story form. I reflect the rhythms of the Christian narrative: the hope of the Triumphal Entry is shattered by the terror of the crucifixion. Fortunately, neither the Gospel nor my journey ends in despair. The seven stories which follow chronicle my pilgrimage into affirmation within the context of the carnival community.

I had to be honest with myself as I crafted this work. One of the responses to the first three volumes of these "autobiographical mythologies" has been that I have presented a classic study of manic depression. I needed to complete that account. As a writer, I had to discover a way of transforming into art my father's rape of his fourteen-year-old son just before his death. What I hope I've accomplished is what an unacknowledged film commentary says about *Saving Private Ryan*: "The hyper-realistic *Ryan* stripped the artifice from film violence and found a horrid poetry at its core."

That second tale is meant as a metaphor for all the terror, abuse and violence rampant in this hurting world. Walk through it in confidence, knowing that you're being awaited by the healing arms of Sharee, Blind Ben See, Ramblin' Rose and that host of carnival outcasts who saved a shattered kid.

The Seashore

The heron led me there.

I was trying to write the Great American Novel on a beach somewhere along the west coast of Florida. But I wasn't really writing. I was wallowing in the muck of brutal images from my childhood and young adolescence. I couldn't shake the anger, the fear and the self-loathing which blindsided me at unexpected moments. Creativity was wiped out by spasms of hate directed toward my dead mindsick daddy.

So, the plan wasn't going to work after all.

I had allowed a month to bury myself beyond all communication with the outside world. A realtor described four walls and a roof "where nobody in his right mind would ever think of going." The description fitted my needs to a T.

She assured me it would probably remain standing another month — if we didn't have a hurricane.

I handed her a hundred bucks and jotted down vague directions. They involved finding a sand-drifted road laid out in a potential Florida paradise which went belly-up. The welcome center had burned to the ground a month after its completion.

I would be staying in the night watchman's "cottage." She assured me it was "furnished." She put vocal quotation marks around the word. Simple needs could be supplied by a Seven-Eleven convenience store. The nearest town was Gibsonton.

I followed her sketchy directions and arrived at the end of a sand-choked road facing a lunar-like landscape. The only sign of life was a great blue heron who circled in the harsh sunlight against a cloudless sky. His shadow on the arid panorama resembled a prehistoric raptor's.

I saw no sign of a "cottage." The heron swooped low and angled toward the beach. I followed.

Cresting the bank flowing down to the sea, I spotted him perched on the roof of a tiny ramshackle structure. Every vestige of paint had weathered off. In the distance, its blue-gray tones flowing into the coloration of the heron made it look like a sculpted base for the great bird.

I entered. Roaches raced for cover. I reached up and pulled a frayed piece of twine dangling from a bare bulb. Twenty-five watts of light exploded the interior into vectored shadows. Spiders skittered for shelter on the ceiling.

I plugged in the rusty refrigerator. It clanked into action. A curtained-off corner hid a stained stool which flushed and a showerhead dribbling cold water into a decaying pan. A filthy little sink completed the bathroom ensemble.

In a corner stood an army cot bedecked with worn sheets, an olive drab blanket and a frayed towel tossed over a caseless pillow. Two plastic milk crates served as a dresser. A graffitied oak table was carved with information about who would do what for how much and phone numbers. A chair with two missing rungs crouched upside down beneath it.

A single-burner hot plate, a scorched saucepan, a set of army surplus silverware and a tin cup made up the kitchen. It was not for nothing that the realtor voiced quotation marks around "furnished."

Yet it would do nicely as a hermitage for facing into and writing out old ghosts and old tales.

I returned to my car and retrieved my laptop computer, an old printer and a suitcase containing paperback poets whom I someday hoped to emulate. The heron shadowed my journey.

Having settled in, I drove to the Seven-Eleven. Not wanting to leave my car in the middle of nowhere, I gave the owner five dollars to let me park it behind the store. I pulled a rucksack from the trunk, loaded it with cornflakes and evaporated milk as preparation for the three-mile hike to my sanctuary in the wilderness. As I left the establishment, I saw a "Frozen Bait" sign. I returned to the counter and bought the heron two containers of shrimp.

For the next week and a half I stared at the computer screen. The memories were there. The intensity of my primal anger at my mindsick daddy paralyzed my fingers poised over the keyboard.

I tried another tack. Whenever my father abused me with horsewhip or fists, he always made me strip. Perhaps essential nakedness would trigger the words. I removed my torn cutoffs and Speedo swim briefs in which I'd been living and sat down on the pillow cushioning the broken chair.

The salt breeze swept over my body. I remembered crouching naked in a field after an accident with a plow horse. I waited for the whip to fall. I felt a drop of water. I looked up. My daddy was bending over me, his eyes brimming with tears. He ground out, "Yer so worthless yuh ain't even worth beatin'!"

As the memory came into sharp focus, I folded my arms over the computer, dropped my head and sobbed for a long, long time.

When I lifted my eyes, I discovered that the monitor finally had something on it. Parts of my anatomy had been in touch with the keyboard. Screen after screen revealed endless combinations of the letters "N," "D" and "G." I choked again. My daddy always told me I was no damn good. Sometimes he'd sneer out verbal shorthand under his breath: "Kid, you're just N-D-G."

The patterns on the computer screen were a taunt from the grave.

The pain was too acute. I threw open the door. The beach was deserted. I raced across the narrow strip of sand outside my rundown *el cheapo* hideaway and plunged into the Gulf, hoping for peace. It never came.

When the day of resolution arrived, it didn't really "break." A strange light crept out of the East and into my consciousness, interrupting the flow of my father-haunted dreams. I took from the crook of my arm my old, worn yellow teddy bear and braced him on the pinstripe pillow. He had been my only gift the first Christmas after my adoption.

Stumbling across the tiny room, I yanked open the ill-fitting door. The sky overhead was jet black. The dome above the sea swirled with roiling wind clouds. Sand devils swayed down the beach.

The ancient heron alighted outside the salt-streaked window, taking refuge against the side of the shack. I reached into the rusting freezer of the clanking refrigerator and pulled out a handful of aging shrimp. I cranked open a screenless pane of glass and extended my fistful of odiferous offerings to the questing beak. The tickle of its bill on the soft flesh of my palm was soothing. In the midst of cyclonic memories of abuse, the unexpected gentleness of the bird's presence was momentarily healing.

As the morning faded into afternoon, I sat staring at the monitor, lost in a reverie which wrapped my spirit in a dull ache. Somehow I had to get the night-toned images written out of my psyche so that something like light might flow in.

By mid-afternoon it was raining heavily, but I could no longer endure the confinement of the cluttered space.

Since I might swim as far as civilization, I pulled a Speedo over my housebound nakedness and inched my way into the storm. I stood in the water's edge, my ankles caressed by the gentle swell of the sea shattered by an amazing downpour. I let the driving rain tear at my flesh like a million needles. There was not a breath of wind — only the deluge plummeting straight down.

The seashore sky was shredded by lightning. My senses were bombarded by deafening thunder. As each peal rolled into the distance, something within me rolled with it. My very life essence dissolved into sky and sand. My knees gave way. I slipped into the soft surge of the ocean and went limp, allowing my floating frame to be carried at the water's will.

The ebbing tide moved me a hundred fifty yards from shore.

A northerly current shifted me parallel to a line of distant palms. I floated on my back, watching the storm disappear toward the west, its clouds slit by scarlet rays from the setting sun.

Far up the otherwise deserted beach I saw two figures which appeared to be carved from driftwood. They flamed in the waning day. As I drifted closer, one came alive and adjusted a robe over the legs of its seated companion.

Their outlines were familiar. A few swift strokes brought me near shore. My body was one with the water.

At that moment, the light's intensity caught the outline of the chair. Golden flashes danced off its surface. They were reflected momentarily in a man's dark glasses.

I was nearly upon them. The sighing of the surf obliterated any sounds of my approach. The woman turned slightly. The raw illumination of the sunset highlighted a knife scar down her cheek and across her throat. It glowed like a rare Inca necklace. The salt spray momentarily blinded me. When my vision cleared, I had floated into the certainty of their presence: Blind Ben See and Ramblin' Rose, who had been people of refuge in my life so many years before.

Ben sat as he always had on his tarnished, peeling golden throne, dreaming of his carnival kingdom alive around him. His black preacherly suit reflected bygone days when the kingdom of the Lord had been his concern. Beneath the coat he wore a golden shirt with an eye embroidered on the left pocket. Dark glasses deepened the mystery surrounding this mythic man who had once ruled a carnival Midway from a Fun House platform.

The reflection of his hunched outline was always distorted by the Mirror of Truth behind him elongating or compressing the images of passersby on their way to the haunted depths of this favored attraction.

As each customer handed him a ticket and prepared to walk through the mouth of the gigantic death's head which masked the entrance of the Fun House, Ben would mutter, "Watch yer step, yer money and yer life."

The surf grounded me. I stood up and walked toward them.

As the sun struggled with the advancing night, I felt like I was back on the carnival lot, the lights of the Star of Bethlehem Ferris wheel washing over me in the dusk.

Rose turned, started and gasped, “My God! It’s Rog!”

She moved to me and took my still-dripping body in her arms. She held me for a long moment. My sun-bronzed cheek rested against the scar. Gripping my shoulders, she extended her arms, saying, “It’s been fifteen years since I seen yuh last. Let me take a good look at yuh.”

Her eyes roved the length of my lanky frame. A crooked grin creased her face as she stared teasingly at my scantily clad groin. A cascade of giggles wreathed her ancient face: “If you ain’t growed into somethin’ else! If I was young again, I’d sing yuh a little chorus of ‘Come Onna’ My House, My Housa’ Come On.”

Ben struggled to his feet and reached toward me. I moved to him. His hands went unerringly to my face. His touch traced my features as if his fingers were moving over a relief map.

“It’s really you, Rog,” he whispered. “What the hell are you doing in this godforsaken place?”

“I’m trying to write a book about you and Sharee and me and my mindsick daddy. If I ever get the words out, maybe I can get the pain out. But my mind screen and my computer screen are both blank. The screen of my heart is scorching with hate. Its smoke obscures everything else in my world.”

I wept. He smiled and said, “Ain’t much has changed since the last time we had this conversation just before you disappeared from the carnival lot after the desecration of Sharee.

“Rose and I often wondered what became of you. I sold the show a long time ago. We decided we’d hang out together. A coupla’ years later we moved over there to Gibtown — what non-carneys call Gibsonton. It’s a place where folk like us winter and retire and die.

“The only thing I saved was my golden throne. Three guys what used to work for me hauled it over to this deserted stretch of beach. Don’t much see anybody unless they mysteriously float up out of the surf. Most every night Rose drives us here 'bout this time. I let the sound of the sea paint memories for me. She can tell me about the sky and the sunset.

"When the nights chill down, we sometimes stretch out on the warm sand under this old buffalo hide robe Tony Great Turtle gave us just before he died. We're getting so feeble we have a little trouble helping one another get up again and stagger across the dunes to Rose's old Chrysler. Some night we're not gonna' make it. We'll just let the tide roll over us. It wouldn't be a bad way to go."

Mist from the sea carried with it bone-chilling cold. My teeth chattered. I queried, "D-D-o you suppose there'd be r-r-room under the r-r-robe for three?"

Rose laughed, "It'd be this woman's wildest dream come true: to bundle on a beach with two of my favorite men in the whole world!"

I helped the ancient figures to the ground. They had faded with the years to feather lightness.

The warmth from the sand and our bodies encased in the antique robe brought contentment while a million stars exploded in the moonless sky.

Ben slipped an arm around me. I felt cocooned in safety. He spoke softly, "Why don't you tell us 'bout this book you're writin' — especially since it's partly about us. We might add a few things, or correct a few things, just to keep you honest."

For the next two hours I talked nonstop until emotional exhaustion halted the flow. A long silence ensued, broken by Blind Ben See's quiet comment, "I have a suggestion, boy — oh, I know, yer a growed man now — even if you do still sound like the carnival kid we knew long ago. Howsomever, you might want to float up here for a few nights and tell us the tales. Maybe we can get you growed up inside as well."

Ramblin' Rose sighed and yawned at the same time: "That was a awe-inspirin', heart renderin' rendition and even kinda' funny at points, but us old folks are gettin' sleepy. It's past our usual bedtime, but I must say, Rog, you're more entertainin' than TV. I've got a better suggestion than Ben's. I don't want to hear no more talk about the stories. I want to hear the real thing. Why don'tcha go back to yer shack and write down quick-like what yuh've just outlined for us. Then late tomorrow afternoon we'll stop for yuh on our way here, and yuh can read us what you've wrote. I've a sneakin' hunch once we git yer writin' pump primed, there'll be no stoppin' yuh. Ben and me can be literary critics."

"Whoa!" I countered. "Where did you pick up fancy language like that?"

She spat back, "We may be carneys, but we ain't dumb."

Chastened, I struggled to my feet and helped Blind Ben and Rose stand, steadying them for a moment while they claimed their balance. I carried the robe as we slowly scaled the low dunes to the potholed road.

We climbed into the ancient Chrysler. After two miles I stopped her at the decaying drive that led to my crumbling hermitage.

From the back seat of the old car I hugged Ben and planted a smacker right in the middle of Ramblin' Rose's scar. They agreed to pick me up about five the next afternoon. As I opened the door, Rose unhooked an object dangling from the rearview mirror.

She said brusquely, "Yuh'd better take this with yuh, kid. It might stir a memory or two — or a meaning or two."

I tenderly held an exquisitely carved eight-inch wooden crucifix with attached Rosary beads. Jesus was straining to pull his hands and feet from the impeding nails. His contorted face reflected the agony of his torment. He was naked. The last time I'd seen it was just before I left the carnival. It was hanging on the wall of my friend Mario's van.

Rose grinned wickedly in the rearview mirror. She commented ruefully, "That's always been my favorite crucifix. The artist was honest enough to carve a real groin without the usual modesty panel. Turn it over."

I followed her instructions. On the reverse was carved a

Christ Triumphant. He was clothed in a royal robe. His arms were curved to embrace the world. His face glowed with a wry grin as if to say, "Surprise! I'm alive!"

Mario'd always had it hanging flat against the wall, agony out. I'd never seen the other side.

I returned the welcoming smile. Rose said quietly, "Well! Yer lookin' almost human again. Jist be careful and don't get too attached to that piece of wood. I want it back when yuh've finished the book."

I kissed her again and carried the trophy gently as I walked down the rutted driveway toward the shack.

The ancient heron was outlined against the Big Dipper. Ben had mentioned Tony Great Turtle, the old Lakota shaman who, so many times before his death, saved a childhood me from despair. Tony had told me that herons contain the souls of the wise ones who have returned to earth on mysterious pilgrimages.

I'd found Blind Ben See and Ramblin' Rose. I was carrying Christ in my hands. Had Tony returned in this heron to share saving wisdom? After a long spell of desperately destructive aloneness, I now began to sense myself surrounded by a cloud of witnesses.

The interior of the shanty was illuminated by light from the monitor. I propped the crucifix, agony out, alongside the bear on my pillow. I slipped out of my Speedo and stepped under the shower's uncertain flow. Without drying myself completely, I moved quickly to the keyboard. For the first time, words flowed.

1

Enter Sharee

The legs of my guilt were long. I wanted to run away.

It was the summer of my sixteenth year. I'd never loved my mindsick daddy. I'd tried to shoot him. Two years ago he'd died from lung cancer. Folks said I was supposed to have loved him. I felt guilty as all hell.

I needed a hiding place where I could be assured I was worth something — but Gletha the Goatlady, my first refuge, was far away. My Hermit Uncle John had fled deep into his Mystery. Tony Great Turtle had died in my arms.

I was working in Axel Torqelson's grocery store in Pheasant Valley, Minnesota, population 782. It was part of a chain of establishments called the Red Owl. From swinging signs huge scarlet birds stared uncomprehendingly at sidewalk passersby. Toddlers hid their eyes from the gargantuan gaze. Citizens seldom said they were going to the Red Owl to pick up a sack of flour. Their destination was always "the Big-Eyed Chick."

Axel was huge. His wife Madge had to cut out his white aprons from extra heavy bed sheets in order to find enough fabric to go around his middle. Axel's favorite corner of his mercantile kingdom was the meat counter. He'd arrive each morning before sunup, resplendent in a fresh, gleaming white apron, "to do a little butchering." He'd dissect a few chickens and saw off great racks of ribs from beef carcasses hanging in the cooler.

Hands bloodied, he'd scratch the large wart on the right

side of his neck. Then, he'd contentedly stroke his fingers over his mountainous belly, leaving gory tracks across the snowfield of his wife's hardwrought handiwork. Kids in town were certain that each dawn he'd encountered a sunrise-shunning vampire fleeing to its coffin in the dank basement of Bunnessen's Funeral Parlor and Furniture Store.

Axel was proud that his folks had been traveling show people. He was fond of proclaiming, "My first resting place was a dresser drawer in Detroit." His mother was an actress. His father, a magician, taught Axel all his tricks. As I became his fill-in behind the counter, he drilled me in the most important of his "sleights of hand."

He said over and over, "The most important fact to remember is that 'the hand is quicker than the eye.'"

I wasn't expected to pull dimes from the nostrils of children or quarters from behind the ears of their elders. That was Axel's stock in trade. And his customers never failed to be amazed.

I was expected to learn the proper use of my thumb. Whenever I threw slices of bologna on the scale, or mounded a mountain of hamburger, or flopped down a limp chicken, I would leave my left thumb to be weighed while lifting my right hand in a grandiose, distracting gesture.

Eyes strayed from the dial of the scale as I pressed steadily, adding a few ounces to every order. When eyes returned, I would announce in my most sincere voice, "This is a mighty fat bird, Miz Trentor. Weighs in at nearly four pounds."

"That'll be fine, Roger. Looks like you picked me a real good one."

With my left thumb unwavering, I'd swoop up the meat with my right hand. Axel would keep a sharp eye on me through the cutting room window.

My "graduation" from the school of meat counter deception happened the day Graciella Grabhorn came in to buy three pounds of hamburger. She was going to bake her famous beer meatloaf for her husband Hank's birthday. Hank was the second largest man in Pheasant Valley next to Axel. Graciella always cooked a little extra for special occasions.

I removed the ground beef with a flourish while requesting that she convey my birthday greetings to Hank, thus further distracting her eagle eye from the numbers on the scale.

The following day Graciella came storming back into the store on the attack. Ignoring seventy-year-old Selma Simpson who'd operated the cash register for fifty years, she confronted Axel, shouting in a voice that could be heard by those having Cokes at Dager's Rexall Drug next door: "Axel, you cheated me. That hamburger musta' been all fat. By the time I set it on the table it had shrunk down so's there wasn't enough for Hank to have a third helping, and it was his birthday yet!"

Axel responded in his most placating voice, "Now, Graciella, there must be some terrible mistake. I tell you what I'll do. I just got a fresh carcass of beef from Ray Evans. Everybody knows he raises the leanest steers in the county. You go on around the store and pick up whatever else you need while I grind you some burger which will be so red it will outshine them flowers on that real purty dress you're wearin' today."

He paused for a moment. A gleam came into his eye. His voice softened. He was obviously doing some of that "thinking on his feet" he always encouraged me to do.

"Graciella, you bake one of your famous beer meatloaves. They're absolutely the best in town by all reports. You invite Madge and me to dinner so's I can check out this here product which I'm selling to the public."

Graciella beamed. "Why don't you let Rog or Selma close up the store, and you and Madge come on by tonight at about 6:30. I always like to have others enjoy my cooking."

She went beaming around the store. I could tell what was being served in addition to the meatloaf from what she was purchasing: a lemon gelatin salad with canned peaches and miniature marshmallows topped with dollops of whipped cream and mayonnaise which the cookbook put out by the ladies at the Roman Catholic Church of St. Ignatius the Lesser said had to be "gently folded together and topped by maraschino cherries."

Dessert would be strawberry shortcake.

Having paid for her purchases, including the three additional pounds of hamburger — Axel had given her full measure so *he* wouldn't be shorted at the dinner table — she waved gaily to him and shouted, "Now, Axel, you and Madge sharpen up your appetites. Hank and I'll see you at 6:30."

I followed her out, carrying heavy bags of groceries to her shiny '48 Ford Roadster. I wondered as we went if there'd be enough strawberries in the quart box to satisfy four huge appetites.

When I returned to the store, Axel grabbed me by the shoulders. Roaring with laughter which Selma always said "could wake the dead at Bunnessen's," he choked out, "You did good, boy. That thumb o' yourn sold me three extra pounds of burger and got me a free meal. By God, I'm going to up your pay two cents. Fifty-two cents an hour is the most I've ever paid a kid."

Rejoicing over my success, I returned to the task which I'd interrupted to carry Graciella's groceries: fluffing strawberries. My concern for the evening's dessert was quite realistic. She had purchased a quart of berries which I'd just "fluffed." The luscious fruit arrived at the store in twelve quart flats. Each individual box was firmly packed and heaped high. My job was to dump a flat of berries out on a counter hidden away in a back room. I'd refill boxes lightly with only a slight rounding on top. We'd gain two or three quarts a flat. That meant extra profit if I did my job right. I'd become an expert "fluffer."

On this particular day in June, I was fluffing away and keeping my eye on the customers as they walked in. There was a little window above the counter. Somebody had stacked Oxydol across the opening. I'd gone out and made a tunnel through the ever-popular laundry detergent. This shadowed the viewing area. I could see out but nobody could see in.

It had been a quiet morning up to now when *she* walked in — the tallest woman I'd ever seen in my life. Her legs went on forever. They were sheathed in tight black slacks. She wore a form-fitting black vest over a gleaming white blouse. The silk fabric flowed to her wrists in great soft folds. Virginal lace at her throat accented her swan-like neck and the long curve of her breasts. Her golden hair was piled high upon her head.

She wore black open-toed slippers with incredibly high heels made of clear plastic — one of those plastics developed especially for the war effort. As she floated down the aisle toward me past the Post Toasties cereal, I thought those heels were the finest items ever created as a result of World War II.

Her brilliant red toenails flashed intermittent passionate fire, as the morning sun streaming through the store's skylight set them ablaze.

She turned abruptly to the right. She was heading for the meat counter. Axel wasn't there! He was having coffee at the Dew Drop Inn with "the downtown boys."

I rushed across the back room and entered the meat cooler through a rear door. In my haste I knocked a haunch of veal from its hook. It plopped to the sawdust covered floor. I emerged behind the scale and tried to assume my best Robert Mitchum matinee idol pose while her attention was distracted by selecting a small jar of peanut butter.

She turned and melted me into befuddled embarrassment with a smile that I'd last seen on the lips of Rita Hayworth enlarged on the screen of the Hollywood Motion Picture Theater on Main Street. In a rich, dark voice which I'd only heard in fantasy conversations between Lancelot and Guenevere, she queried, "Could you serve me a quarter pound of minced ham?"

I mumbled something hideously inane like, "Thank you for that fine order, ma'am."

I sliced the requisite amount and placed it on the scale — leaving my magic thumb suspended in the air. It was slightly over a quarter pound. Removing the meat, I gallantly tossed an extra slice on the stack, just for good measure.

Her eyes glowed in my direction. My trembling fingers melted into thumbs as I tried to tape up her package. She said duskily, "Let me help you."

She leaned toward me. The sensuous scent accosting my nostrils wafted straight to her snow-white skin from southern magnolia blossoms. Strains of Stephen Foster throbbed in my heartstrings. The neatly taped package emerged a work of art.

Lowering her incredibly long lashes, she whispered, "Thank you for your generosity."

She headed for the fruit bin and reached for a box of strawberries. I was instantaneously at her side, assuring her, "I just got a new shipment of fresher berries. Don't you bother with those."

I rushed to the back room, emerging a moment later with a quart of elegant berries — unfluffed! I bore them to her as if I were carrying the fabled Grail itself. She received my offering with queenly modesty and headed for the cash register with her three items.

Selma stepped into the aisle and looked her over from head to toe, her face distorted with evident disgust. In her best Baptist voice laced with self-righteous prophetic indignation she spat out, "I don't wait on no floozies!"

She stomped off toward the back room, her runover carpet slippers slapping stentoriously on the slivered floor. *Her* heels were *not* made from clear plastic.

I rushed to the register before the arrival of the beautiful apparition. She had paused to stare blankly at Selma's disappearing back.

Turning and placing her items on the counter, she quickly discovered I had a problem. I didn't know how to operate the cash register. I picked up a stub pencil and toted up her bill on the side of a brown paper bag.

She opened a small alligator purse suspended from her shoulder by a snakeskin strap. Trying to cover my discomfiture at not being able to use the machine, she said tactfully, "I'm three cents short of the exact amount."

Sly laughter crinkled at the corners of her cupid's bow mouth as she continued, "I guess I'll just have to give you back part of one of these gigantic berries."

She lifted the largest to her lips. Her perfect teeth sliced it daintily in half. She sucked the fruit into her mouth and savored it for a long moment. Her tiny tongue caught a drip of juice about to descend from the half in her fingers. She languidly licked the cut expanse to prevent further extrusion of liquid.

Then she raised the remaining half to my lips, bite side first!

I took in the offering, reaching my lips a bit beyond the berry so they might momentarily caress the soft surfaces of the servant fingertips.

This paradisical viand could not possibly have emerged from the mere soil of the Jones farm outside of town where Axel had supposedly purchased it. The touch of this grocery store goddess had transformed it into rare passion fruit straight from the Garden of Eden itself.

I placed her three items in a small bag and pleaded, "Please, allow me to carry your groceries to your car."

She hesitated. "That would be most kind, but my vehicle is some distance away."

I automatically breathed out, "G-o-o-d!"

I wanted all seven hundred and eighty-two inhabitants of Pheasant Valley — and everyone in the surrounding township, the extended county, the state of Minnesota, the entire Americas, all global neighbors, even dwellers on distant planets, to see me, Rog Robbennolt, object of derision who had never had a date, to see *me* walking in the shadow of quintessential beauty.

Whistles and catcalls trailed us. We walked proudly together. We neared City Park. She pointed to a gigantic van on the other side of the green expanse.

She stated matter-of-factly, "That's our destination."

As we neared the great vehicle, a scene painted on the side floated into view. A gigantic silver full moon shone down into a jungle clearing. Ladies were dancing in its light. They weren't wearing much in the way of clothing. The tiny bits of essential covering were zebra-striped. Arching over the entire scene in brilliant gold lettering whose style was usually reserved for illuminated monastic manuscripts were the words ***ZE BRA***.

I gasped. I was staring at a van which certainly housed a troupe of "cooch dancers," a girlie show on its way to join up with a touring company — most likely Blind Ben See's Carnival of Wonders, which had been missing such an attraction when it played our town three days before.

I was led to the far side of the van. She turned to me and said, "My name's Sharee. What's yours?"

My mouth was so dry I could hardly speak. My voice squeaked as I muttered, "Rog."

She smiled and continued, "I'm on my way to join Blind Ben in Maple River. Celeste and Lola, who also dance in the show, will meet me there."

She reached for her groceries with her left hand and with her right surrounded my quivering fist cramped from grasping the bag. She looked me in the eyes and said softly, "Rog, I think you are just about the politest man I have ever met."

She disappeared through the door into inner mystery.

I floated around to the other side of the van. She'd called me a man! Nobody had ever called me a man before. I'd certainly try to be one — though I wasn't quite sure how.

I lost myself in the jungle scene. My vision was absorbed into the great silver orb. Without warning, the face of my mindsick daddy floated to the surface of the full moon.

The Seashore

I reached the end of the tale. I was astounded! Pages and pages from my past flowed across the screen. I stumbled to my feet. Every joint cried out from the tension generated by the immobility of my story-centered focus.

The battered Little Ben alarm clock on the windowsill caught a beam of moonlight. It was 2:30 A.M. My body needed the healing embrace of water.

I threw open the door and reveled in a moonlit sprint to the sea's edge. I shattered the glassy surface with a belly flop. I stroked hard, discovering refreshment from the salty tang. Two hundred yards out I flipped on my back and floated, letting the tide drift me to shore like a bit of misshapen driftwood.

In the midst of the unusually still water, a hurricane wrenched my psyche. I had to tell the heart of the story — though my mother must have said a half-dozen times a day, "Don't you ever, ever tell anybody about your mindsick daddy."

My butt dragged on the sand beneath the shallows. I waded to shore and let the wind dry my body. The soft air caressed me into action. I had to untie the knot in my gut before sleep would come.

I loped across the sand. Pain surfaced in my left arch. I bent down and discovered a long, rusted spike imbedded in the beach. It had scratched the soft flesh of my foot. I dug it out and was about to hurl it into gnarled bushes when a use for it flashed into my mind. I picked up a small rock that had been a part of the old foundation.

I entered the shack and pounded the spike into the wall high above my computer. I picked up my worn teddy bear and dangled him from the nail by a red ribbon he wore jauntily around his neck. I hung the crucifix by its Rosary beads. It swayed below the bear in the sea breeze flowing through the grim room.

I stared at the ensemble: the spike tinged with my blood, mingling with the blood from the torn flesh of Jesus, in company with the saving bear, my enduring icon of hope.

I headed for the keyboard. I was stopped by a sound: the rhythmic squeak of hinges as the shack's ill-fitting door swung in the soft sea breeze. My body began to move back and forth as the image of our old oak rocking chair shaped itself in my memory. My mother had crocheted an elegant antimacassar which graced its back. The stitches shaped a leaping stag and the words, "God Bless Our Happy Home."

When Dad would reach the depths of his "darknesses," he'd always rock in that chair hour after hour, days without end.

My fingers began scurrying over the keyboard. Pain flowed out.

The Fist, The Rifle, The Rape, The Rope

Each scraggly whisker was gold-tipped by the full moon shining through the cobwebbed window. My mindsick daddy's head lolled against the back of the old rocking chair. He looked like he was already dead. His thin lids barely covered his bulging eyeballs.

He was a perfect target. I gripped the rafter with my knees. His favorite Remington deer rifle was cradled in the crook of my right arm.

All at once he began to s-l-o-w-l-y rock back and forth. There was a slight bump by the side of his chair. The left rocker encountered the slender tip of a horse whip snaking along the rough concrete floor of the corncrib alleyway.

I'd have to aim carefully. I had no fear of missing. I'd dropped many a leaping jackrabbit.

I had to kill my daddy. If I didn't he was going to make a terrible mistake and kill me.

My folks had adopted me when I was three-and-a-half. My father's abuse deepened the older I got and the worse his depressions became. Mom and I always hid him during his darknesses so folk wouldn't see his other side. Now, at fourteen, I had endured the worst incident of my short life.

At the time we were living in a corncrib in southern Minnesota. My places of refuge from childhood were no longer available. I felt the spirits of Gletha the Goatlady, my Hermit Uncle John and Tony Great Turtle hovering in my heart. Without the memories of their love I would have given up long ago. However, they couldn't hold back Dad's whip or fist — or the wanton destructiveness of his tongue. He'd long ago convinced me I was "no damned good." They couldn't keep him from doing to my mother whatever it was that caused her screams to erupt in the night.

I was desperately alone — except for two friends who never left me. Each night when I undressed I took the little worn yellow teddy bear from the pocket of my bib overalls. He'd lived there since he'd arrived as my only gift that first Christmas after I'd been brought from the Owatonna orphanage to this abode of terror.

I'd put the bear on the pillow, snuggle into the goosedown mattress and await the arrival of my unexpected buddy.

The ten by twenty-four foot concrete alley which was our living space was flanked by two gigantic slatted cribs of drying corn. Mom had hung a burlap potato sack as a curtain across one corner where she and Dad slept.

My rusted iron cot was at the opposite end. It was exposed to anyone who happened through. I kept my few belongings in an orange crate beneath my bed.

A wood cookstove and a fuel-oil powered heater for winter stood in the center. They were flanked by a kitchen cabinet, a worn stand holding a dishpan and water bucket and a small table at which the three of us ate our meager fare. In a far corner was a chipped white icebox, cooled by a block from a neighbor's icehouse, that chilled butter, eggs, milk, meat and cream. This domestic arrangement was completed by a cream separator standing aloof in the corner at the foot of my cot. Dad's rocking chair was set beneath the only window.

Rats abounded. They were drawn by the corn. Every night a soft rustle was heard throughout the crib. Gray shadows intersected moonrays on the rough concrete floor.

Early one morning I awoke sensing something incredibly soft curled up against my left cheek. For a moment I thought it was my bear until I realized I was clutching him in my right hand.

I turned my head slightly. May morning light crept into the

crib's essential darkness. I saw the outline of a huge rat nestled into my graying feather pillow. As I moved, it pressed its back more tightly against my face.

The muscles in my fourteen-year-old legs cramped in terror. I gasped for breath. I was experiencing the same panic I'd felt when my daddy had hung me naked on a horse stall wall while trying to teach me not to play.

I began to focus on the warmth emanating from the animal. My mind whirled back to the time when Gletha the Goatlady had run my thumb down the incredibly soft fur on the throat of a timber wolf and commented: "Remember, Rogee. If you can be in touch with what you fear most, you'll prob'ly discover inside it something that's healing and beautiful."

I lifted my head. The creature rolled on its back into the hollow of my pillow. The light quickened. Before me was an old male rat with three paws. Crusty scarring marred his right front haunch. He'd most likely chewed off his leg while caught in a trap.

The muscles in my own legs relaxed. My breath flowed freely. I slowly rose to a sitting position on the edge of the cot. The rat never stirred.

I thought, "Dad's right. I'm no damn good. I'm down to havin' as my only friends a crippled rat and a worn teddy bear."

I pulled on my jock strap — the only underwear my daddy'd let me wear. He didn't want anybody to risk seeing even the outlines of my shameful private parts.

I slipped on my overalls and snapped the bear into the expansive bib. The rat awakened, turned over and eyed me quizzically from two brown beads perched on either side of his long nose. I tiptoed on my bare feet over the cold cement to the kitchen cupboard. I opened the bread drawer. It's ancient wood emitted a loud shriek. I stood stalk still, fearing my folks might awaken. There was no sound from behind the burlap.

I broke off a piece of bread from a stale loaf. I tiptoed back and put the offering at the tip of the rat's nose. He devoured it greedily. He seemed to wink at me knowingly before he disappeared off the side of my bed.

I stepped into the cold morning. The frigid dew on the grass anesthetized my toes. A single star gazed at me from the brightening sky. I breathed in through my nose and out through my mouth as Tony Great Turtle, the old Lakota shaman, had taught me. I tried to breathe in the star's waning light, reminding myself I had sacred light inside me, even though it was always on the verge of being snuffed out by my daddy's brutality. I felt a twinge of hope.

It did not last long. As I headed to the barn to milk our three cows, I heard my mom starting a corncob fire in the cook stove. Midway through my ministrations to the final beast, I heard my father shout, "Damn it all, Mary, you've scorched my toast again!"

Slamming the screen door, he slouched toward the old Fordson tractor. He turned the crank. The engine chugged into sluggish action, encouraged by an onrush of profanity. My daddy's interior darkness was rapidly descending once again. I heard him drive angrily toward the field where tiny shoots of new corn awaited their first plowing. Blinded as he was by his anger, occasional rows of tender green growth would be killed by the misguided, slashing plow.

I carried the milk to the corncrib. Stepping into the dusky interior, I saw the outline of my mother by the stove. She was staring blankly down. The only sound was the sizzle of her tears on the hot stove lids. She reached for a wet dishrag and polished offending crumbs from the stovetop.

I sat down at the table and spread strawberry jam on a piece of the disputed toast. It tasted to me like the food of the gods I was reading about at school in *Bullfinch's Mythology.*

Mom sank down at the far end of the table. She spoke softly: "I'm gittin' outta' here for awhile. Millie Hearthfull is about to deliver her eighth. Her no-good husband, Cado, lets the kids run wild. I'll stay over a few days and take care of things there. You mind yer daddy."

She stepped behind the burlap hanging and packed a few belongings in a small apple basket. Leaving, she paused at the screen door, turned and gave me those final instructions she'd bound me with for eleven years: "Don't you ever tell, boy. Don't you ever tell the things he's done in private. Don't you ever tell."

She disappeared down the gravel road into the light of the rising sun.

I ridded up the ravages of the breakfast terror and washed dishes in warm water from the stove's reservoir. Far in the distance I heard the omnipresent growl of my daddy's tractor.

What could I do to really please him, to make him proud of me, to detour his darkness when he came in for lunch? If I worked extra hard at something, that might do it. A single shaft of sunlight passed over the face of the Little Ben windup alarm clock standing on a wooden nail keg just outside the burlap hanging. The last thing my father did each night was to set it at 5:00 A.M.

It was now 6:30. If I headed for the garden and carefully cultivated the emerging early lettuce, radishes, peas and potatoes, he'd be proud of me.

A decrepit hoe was leaning against a fence post by the rotting wooden garden gate. It's handle was roughened by long use and exposure to the elements. My daddy would never let Mom and me put it inside. It always had to be in sight. Otherwise we might forget to care for the vegetables, causing us all to starve to death.

A landscape painter might have created a memorable work of art after viewing my morning's hoeing. The sides of valleys to catch the rain sloped gently upward to even crests from which emerged the tender leaves of the infant plants glowing in the warm May light.

I unsnapped the pocket of my bib overalls and removed my bear so he might observe my masterwork. His one button eye winked approvingly. I lifted his left ear to my right eye, letting it absorb the rivulet of sweat momentarily blinding me.

I heard the faraway sound of the tractor sputter to silence. My father's hoarse swearing shattered the late spring softness as he wangled the ancient engine back to reluctant life. I watched the distant enraged figure kick clods of earth. Striding back and forth, his heavy boots stomped the life out of tender shoots.

Suddenly, I felt at one with the crushed corn. I sank to the warm earth. Each of his staccato steps scored the index of my pain. The very cells of my body winced as they remembered blows from fist, whip and booted foot.

He paused and gave the tractor's crank a furious turn. The engine coughed into sporadic action. I staggered to my feet as the images receded.

I headed for the pump to draw a drink of cold water. Placing my palm on the iron handle, I felt a flash of pain. I turned over my hands and stared at the rising blisters. The weathered hoe had done its work, marking my obdurate father's will on my flesh.

The cast of the sun indicated it must be about 11:00 A.M. My daddy would demand his lunch at high noon. Maybe if I fixed something he truly loved to eat, the demon driving him would be temporarily exorcised.

I knew what I'd do. I'd bake him light, flaky baking powder biscuits. On rare occasions he was soothed by such a special offering.

I headed for the corncrib. I lit a glowing fire in the cookstove so the oven would quickly heat. I stirred together flour, salt and baking powder. With two knives I carefully cut in the requisite amount of fresh butter until the soft dough emerged in bits the size of peas. Instead of the usual milk, I dribbled rich cream into the dough until it barely clung together. I sprinkled a faint dusting of flour on a bread board. I kneaded the biscuits for a few moments. The dough soothed my blistered hands. I flattened the pastry into an oblong with an ancient rolling pin. Thinking bigger might be better, I didn't roll them quite as thin as my mother did.

I got out a blackened cookie sheet and the battered cutter. I carefully spaced the rounds of dough in even rows on the old pan which had seen similar service for a half-century. I placed them in the hot oven.

I pulled a cast iron frying pan onto a front stove lid. I crisply fried strips of salt pork, poured the fat into a Campbell's Pork and Beans can on a stoveside orange crate and added a jar of drained home-canned green beans. I brewed fresh coffee. I would set before my father a feast which would have calmed the Bible's mad King Saul.

I heard the tractor crawling into the shade of the storm-twisted barn. I screwed a smile on my face and ran out to greet my scowling father as he shuffled his way toward the smell of baking biscuits.

"D-D-Dad, c-c-come to the garden. See wh-wh-what I've d-d-done special this morning."

Without responding, he grudgingly shifted his direction. He stared for a moment at patterns of moist earth and bright green leaves. He exploded, "What the hell have yuh gone and did? Yuh've mounded the rows so high the first hot sun will burn up the plants. Yuh've gone and ruined the whole damned garden! We're on our way to the poorhouse fer sure."

The blisters in my palms tingled.

He continued, "I sure hope to hell yer Ma has slopped together somethin' halfway decent for lunch."

I hesitated for a moment, then stammered out, "Sh-Sh-She's g-g-gone over to the Hearthfull's. Millie's about t-t-to d-d-deliver. She'll b-b-be with 'em a f-f-few days. B-B-But don't worry, D-D-Dad, I'll take care of you real good. I've got l-l-lunch ready for us r-r-right n-n-now."

He turned in wordless rage over Mom's desertion and headed toward the corncrib. I ran before him. The aroma filling our living space overcame the musty smell of drying corn and rat dung.

I pulled out the pan of biscuits. They were beautiful, having risen to extraordinary heights and browned to burnished gold. I lifted a plate from the warming oven and neatly stacked the delectable bread on it. In order to keep them warm, I covered them with a fresh white dish towel embroidered in the corner with a kitten hanging out laundry under the word "Monday" outlined in tiny pink roses. I quickly served up the piping hot beans and salt pork.

As he entered, he slammed the screen door, muttering under his breath something about wishing he'd never married "that goddamn woman." I poured some hot water from the teakettle into the washpan on the stand, expecting him to leaven it with a dipperful of cold water from the bucket. Instead, he plunged his field-soiled hands into the hot liquid.

I'm sure the neighbors a mile away heard his outcry: "What the hell are yuh trying' to do? Scald the shit out of me?"

I leaped to his side and poured a dipperful of cool water over his quivering hands. He patted them tentatively with the worn towel. I made no attempt to apologize. Matters would simply worsen.

He slouched to the table and snatched a biscuit from the stack. He split it open and knifed off the peak of the small mountain of butter I'd churned the day before. His face softened a bit as he watched it melt into the warm pastry. He topped it with a dollop of gooseberry jam. He devoured the biscuit in two enormous gulps and reached for another.

His hand encountered the ungainly offering which I'd clumped together out of leftover bits of dough separating the other circles. He didn't bother to open the outsized biscuit. He simply layered on butter and jam. He opened his mouth wide and closed his teeth over an enormous bite. The beatific look engendered by his first encounter with my baking was replaced by wanton rage. He threw the remaining pastry in my face. Crumbs exploded in my right eye. It once again needed the ministrations of the bear's ear.

He spat the offending bread across the table straight at me. It splattered across my overall's bib. He rose to his feet, knocking his chair across the room as he shouted, "What the hell are yuh trying to do? Poison me? That biscuit was raw on the inside! Can'tcha do one goddamn thing right?"

He seized me by the suspenders and pulled me to my feet. "Yer nothin' but a little worthless piece a' shit! I've got a responsibility to teach yuh not to screw up, perticularly since yer almost a man."

He glanced at the horsewhip which ever hung on the wall. He whispered softly, "Strip, kid."

I'd been through this so many times before. I wearily dropped my overalls. My shaking fingers caught the snap on the bib pocket. As the garment sank to the cracked cement floor, the head of the teddy bear appeared, observing the ensuing scene through his single button eye.

I stepped from the stack of faded fabric and turned my back on my daddy so that he wouldn't see my "shameful parts" when I skinned out of my jock strap. As I bent over, a heavy boot to my buttocks sent me sprawling. My breath was knocked out as I slammed into the cement.

Having been blindsided by his brutality, I didn't curl in my usual protective ball. I waited for the first blow to fall. The cold from the concrete seeped into my bloodstream.

When the expected slash did not occur, I turned my head in time to see him step to the table and plunge the middle finger of his right hand into the summitless mountain of butter. He turned quickly and rammed the well-lubricated digit up my rectum. The broken fingernail, caked with cornfield soil, tractor grease and barnyard manure tore at the tender tissue.

I crab-scrabbled away from the pain. He used my momentum to shove me into the wall with his impaling fist. A protruding nail scraped the soft flesh in front of my left ear. Warm blood pooled in the hollow. I could hear my heart pounding.

He removed his finger but remained astraddle my battered body. The liquid in my ear softened the sound of his voice as he ground out, "That's just a little taste of what yer gonna' git if you ever screw up again, perticularly now when that worthless woman has run off and I can't git it when I want it."

I wasn't sure what he meant. My eyes fell to his groin. His loose overalls were ballooned out over a full erection. Images of barnyard bulls servicing obedient cows flashed across my mindscreen. I knew exactly what he meant.

He abruptly left me, closing the screen door with a wood-shattering slam. I lay sobbing softly. With the index finger of my blistered left hand I began tracing patterns along the cracks in the concrete, outlining faraway continents of contentment where I would never be shattered again — where I could feel worthy and real.

I struggled up and leaned on my left elbow. My eye caught the outline of my father's prize Remington rifle resplendent on its rack of deer antlers. The solution to my terror presented itself. I'd shoot my daddy.

I got the rest of the way to my feet. I swayed dizzily for a moment as the pain slashed at me. I stepped to the stove and ladled warm water from the reservoir to the washpan. I soaked a piece of torn Turkish towel and gently sponged the blood from my ear and groin.

I put on my clothes and began clearing the table. I stared at the imprint of my father's finger in the butter mountain. It looked like a volcanic core which I'd learned about in Mr. Sonnenberg's eighth grade science class. For a moment I felt the heat of molten lava in my bowels.

I picked up the plate of golden biscuits which had failed as a peace offering. I carefully carried it through the screen door, now hanging limply from its hinges, another victim of my father's violence.

I walked to the hog yard and flung the oven-gilded nuggets in a wide half-circle. They fell to the muck and gleamed there in the light of high noon until the snarling pack of swine descended. Amid frenzied squabbling, the biscuits were devoured.

I looked into the distance and watched the tractor crawl slowly through the cornfield like a potato bug. The fine flame of my anger rose. I stared at the plate in my hand. My father found it in a sack of oatmeal. It had been a dividend. He hid it until Christmas and gave it to my mother. I raised it high above my head and shattered it on a rock which steadied the sagging gate of the hog yard. Having been destroyed, I had an overwhelming desire to destroy. As I stared at bits of china rose petals scattered among thistles and milkweed, I didn't really feel any better.

On my way back to the corncrib I paused at the garden. A few brief hours ago it was a source of pride. My daddy's slashing words and the burning between my legs transformed the neat rows into the landscape of hell.

Late afternoon, Dad rolled the sputtering tractor into the

shade of the moldering barn. I sat in his chair by the window reading Horatio Alger's *Jed, the Poorhouse Boy*, dreaming of the day I could run away and become rich and famous.

My father entered silently, deep in his "darkness." As I suspected, no food was required tonight. He slipped behind the burlap curtain. I had gone over to my dark corner as I usually did when I prepared for sleep. I'd stripped and stretched out on my bed, warily watching for my dad. After a few minutes he shoved the curtain aside and emerged from my folks' bedroom area, clad only in the shorts my ma made for him from flour sacks. He took the horsewhip from the wall and threw it to the floor at his side. He sank into the great oak rocking chair, his right hand clutching his crotch. He muttered over and over in a rhythm I'd heard from Egyptian priests in "Aida" one Saturday afternoon when I'd snuck a listen to the Metropolitan Opera on the battery-operated radio: "She's gone — she's gone and left me — the goddamn woman's gone and left me."

Darkness fell. The full moon rose. I snuggled my bear. The old rat arrived. I whispered my plan to the two of them. I'd quietly lift the Remington rifle off the antlers, climb the rickety ladder to a rafter and shoot him. My tortured imagination assured me that if I shot him from above, the bullet would pass through more of his body. If his blood spattered, I'd be out of range.

I rose and pulled on my overalls so I'd have some protection between my bruised butt and the wood. I stuffed the bear quickly into the bib. His single eye peered over the pocket edge. The old rat perched on the graying pillow. As he sank into the goose down, he appeared to be emerging from a tunnel in soft earth.

The shaky ladder to the top of the drying cages held. I found myself astride a rafter ready to take aim at my rocking daddy's head illumined by the soft gold light of the full moon flowing through the spiderwebbed window. I slowly raised the gun and began to capture the rocking rhythm of the tortured man. My blistered finger burned against the harsh steel of the trigger. I was about to focus Dad squarely in the gun sights when the soft flesh on the underside of my right wrist brushed the bear.

I began to cry. My body was torn by uncontrollable sobs. I reached out with my left hand and grabbed a crib slat to keep myself from falling. My grip on the rifle loosened. It fell on my cot below, barely missing the old rat who quickly slithered down between the bed and the wall. The gun bounced to the floor with a clatter. It did not fire.

In dumb amazement, I perched precariously on the beam as my sobs subsided. My daddy was right. I was no damn good. I couldn't even bring myself to kill him after his noontime threat. I needed more time to strengthen my resolve. Dad would sit in the chair for days.

I climbed down the ladder. I reached the bottom rung. A rotting handhold gave way. I fell flat on my back.

Struggling to my feet, I returned the gun to the antlers and headed for my cot. I placed the bear gently on my pillow. I pulled off my overalls and eased myself down on my belly. A few moments later the old rat crept into his accustomed place by my cheek. I was surprised that he trusted me enough to return, having been nearly done in by the falling gun.

I whispered my plan for the following night. The rat and the bear agreed.

I fell into a deep sleep. I dreamed I was in Jerusalem. Jesus was making his triumphal entry. Rather than riding an ass, he was astride a unicorn. Doll-like, I rode in front of him, behind the great beast's horn. My blistered hands healed at the touch of the golden protuberance. The fire in my groin cooled.

Suddenly I was torn from my perch by rough hands. Voices shouted that I wasn't good enough to be near the Lord. Jesus leaned down and whispered, "I'll be with you later." His voice was lost amidst hosannas.

Cloth was being tied around my face. I couldn't breathe. I couldn't cry out.

I awoke with a start. A rough hand was spread over my eyes and nose. My pillow was being stuffed into my mouth. A naked body pinioned me to the bed. It was my daddy tearing me apart because of his anger at my mother.

I was being lacerated deep inside. Dad paused for a moment, screaming. I felt him fling his hand out and heard a thud across the room. At first I thought he'd thrown my teddy bear. Then, I was aware of my bear cushioning my privates from every rupturing thrust.

His speed increased. Bile rose in my throat. I'd eaten no food since morning toast. He cried out again. A volcanic eruption of moist pain drove me to the edge of oblivion. He collapsed fully on me for a moment and then withdrew. I saw his naked outline in the moonlight as he slouched heavily across the room. He muttered his priestly dirge: "She's left me — she's gone and left me — the goddamn woman's gone and left me."

He disappeared behind the burlap hanging. I lolled my head over the side of the bed and retched. Nothing came.

I lay motionless for a long time, drifting on a sea of pain. I wondered where Jesus had been. He promised me he would protect me. No, wait a minute. That's not what he really said. He said he'd be with me. I thought Jesus'd make me feel whole, feel good about myself. But he let my daddy violate me. Dad had finally done it — made me feel ultimately "no damn good," good only as something to be used. No Jesus with any power would let that happen. But then I remembered: It was a dream Jesus. Maybe, I thought, that's the only kind of Jesus there really is.

I reached down to retrieve my bear. My hand encountered the slimy stickiness of blood and semen. I placed him at the edge of my pillow. I wished the old rat would come and nestle by my cheek. I feared he was scared away forever.

A gray dawn forced leaden light through the filthy window. I tried to move. Every inch of my body hurt. Most of the pain was in my mind.

Suddenly, violent coughing erupted from behind the burlap — gurgling and gagging such as I'd only heard when we slit the throat of a butchered steer now roiled out from my tortured father. Between onslaughts of deathlike rattles he cried out weakly, "Kid, git yerself in here."

I lay motionless. Another fit of coughing disturbed the

morning stillness. Maybe he'd die on his own. Maybe I wouldn't have to kill him. Something deep inside me wanted to.

His voice rose again in a high-pitched scream. It shaped itself into my mother's name: "M—A—R—Y—E—E—E!"

I pulled myself up from my cot and staggered toward the gasping man. I did not see the shorts he'd dropped the night before on his way to attack me. I caught my feet in them and plunged to the concrete. The cool floor felt good to my fevered body. Maybe I'd just lay there and let him choke to death.

He called to me again between gasps: "Please . . . come . . . kid . . . . I didn't . . . mean . . . to . . . hurt yuh . . . . Please . . . c—o—m—e."

The final word trailed off weakly into the dawn.

I struggled to my hands and knees and crawled toward the sound. A blister on my left palm exploded, leaving small patches of moisture on the cement each time I moved. I reached the burlap hanging. I grasped it and pulled myself to a standing position. As I was about to regain my balance, the rod holding it in place collapsed. The curtain on that inner sanctum of terror was down forever.

My father lay on a blood-soaked pillow. The slab wall by the bed was splattered with scarlet. Each time he coughed, more blood flowed from the corners of his mouth. He quieted for a moment and whispered, "Go git Oly and Art. They'll take me to the hospital in Pheasant Valley. Then . . . find yer ma."

Oliver and Arthur Atreus were brothers who raised pigs the next farm over. They'd never married and were the shyest men in Sunrise Township. On the other hand, they'd do anything for anybody.

My strength was returning. Dad was quiet. Daylight brightened. As I moved toward my cot, I saw that my thighs were clotted with blood. There was no time to clean up. I pulled on my overalls and moved as fast as I could across the fields. With every step my groin remembered my daddy's thrusts.

The Atreus brothers came at once. They hovered over my father, clucking at the blood. He was asleep. They folded back his bedclothes. Oly gasped, "Goodness gracious! Frank's even bloody down there."

They turned their backs quickly so they need not look at his privates. Art said apologetically, "We thought he'd be dressed and ready to go. We didn't mean to see him like that. Rog, I think you'd better take some warm water from the reservoir and sponge the blood off all over. It's better that family do things like that than it be done by neighbors."

I covered him once again. His breath was coming easier. He didn't waken.

Oly turned back to him. He gasped as he spotted what I had missed: "Great God! Look at the back of poor Frank's right hand. He's been half ate to death by rats. Oh, that's what happens to poor folk who live in corncribs."

The back of my father's hand was covered with rat bites. One laceration had left a ridge of jagged flesh as if the teeth had been yanked from their hold on the skin. I remembered his scream in the night and the sound of something soft hitting the wall by the cream separator. The old rat had tried his best to save me.

I moved woodenly to the stove and filled the washpan with warm water. I dropped a piece of Turkish towel in the pan and headed for Dad's bedside. He had awakened. He lay unmoving as I washed his blood from his wan face, his thinning hair, his bare shoulders and the back of his right hand.

I folded back the covers and gently sponged my blood from his genitals.

Art came over, carrying my father's shorts: "I found these in the middle of the floor. It looks to me like he probably got feeling real sick, tried to walk to your bed to wake you up, couldn't make it and lost these on his way back."

I said nothing.

I slipped the shorts up over his thin legs. Oly and Art helped him finish dressing. A bit of strength began to rise in him. They helped him to their car. His final plea was a gentle word: "Please . . . please find yer ma and git her to Pheasant Valley."

Tears were streaming down his face. I promised I would.

I watched the Atreus' old Model T Ford disappear down the

washboarded gravel road. A cloud of dust glowed golden in the morning light.

Returning to the corncrib, I poured the bloody water on the roots of the wild rose which struggled to grow by the door. I refilled the pan and slipped out of my overalls. I turned in front of a long cracked mirror my mother had hung on a studding behind the wash basin. My buttocks and upper thighs were mapped with rivulets of dried blood.

I washed as best I could, cringing as I tried to soak the blood from the torn tissues at the point of my father's entry.

I slipped on my jock strap and overalls. There was no hurry going for my mother. I would do the chores first. I mixed skimmed milk and meal for the voracious pigs, threw cracked corn to the chickens and gathered their scattered eggs. The three cows gazed at me in dumb appreciation when I appeared to relieve their swollen udders.

I carried the milk to the corncrib and prepared to run it through the cream separator. It was then I found the dead body of the old rat. I picked him up and held him gently. He'd tried his best to distract my father. In his anger, passion and pain Dad had flung him to his death.

I laid him on the pillow. The bear was still where I had put him during the darkest night of my life. In the dim light of day I saw that he too was caked with dried blood. I lay down between my two friends. Repeated blows from my father's fist had punched a hole through my heart. I wondered if it would ever heal.

Carrying the body of the old rat to a lilac bush at the edge of the cornfield, I buried him beneath it, carefully mounding the earth. I walked over by the pig yard where I had shattered the plate. I reassembled a ceramic rose and placed it in the soft dirt over my friend's grave.

I returned to the corncrib to minister to my bear. Filling the washbasin with cold water, I squeezed liquid through him again and again until it finally ran clean.

I took a hammer and a nail from my father's toolbox. Tenderly taking the bear outside, I laid him on a low branch of a gigantic elm. I pounded the nail into the great trunk. I hung the bear out to dry by his frayed scarlet neck ribbon.

Hanging there, his arms outstretched, he looked like a worn, woolly crucifix. Maybe Jesus *had* been with me after all.

My daddy died on his own after six months in the Pheasant Valley Community Hospital, helped along by lung cancer. Mom said she needed to be near him. Leaving the farm in the hands of renters, we moved to town.

Mother sat by his bedside, holding his hand day after long day. I could hardly endure going into his room.

I felt completely alone in town. One day, I was sitting on the back steps of our rented house. An ancient black alley cat crept close. I gently stroked his ears and the top of his nose. The rest of him was too dirty and sore-covered to snuggle.

It felt good to touch something soft and alive. Every night he would stalk me. I wouldn't know he was around until I felt his claws digging into my leg. I talked to him at some length about my feelings. The bear appreciated someone else sharing my burdens.

Mom and I needed money. I lied about my age and entered the workforce of a poultry processing plant. My job was to stand next to the "sticker," who slit the throats of chickens immediately after they were hung upside down on the conveyor chain. I tore out the large wing feathers before they went into the steam vats, where great rotating drums lined with what looked like door springs cleaned off most of the feathers.

Since the birds were still flopping wildly when they passed me, I'd end the day covered with blood. At night when I'd strip to clean up, I'd looked at my disfigured body in the looking glass above the sink. My image would immediately be transplanted to a corncrib mirror. The battered, bloody kid who stared out was me. I wondered if I'd ever forget.

We had no telephone. A neighbor lady, Mattie Gringstead, came to tell us my daddy'd died. When she was given the news, my mother's scream was heard all up and down the block. Folks came running. She stood keening loudly, "My mate is dead. My mate is dead. What'll I ever do without my mate?"

I tried to put an arm around her. She ignored me. I slipped through the crowd of gawking onlookers drawn by the sights and sounds of death and retreated to the back steps.

I couldn't focus. Swirling images invaded my mind. Every cell in my body simultaneously storied each of my father's blows. I tried to cry. Tears were nonexistent. I tried to vomit. Nothing came. Laced through all my responses was deep-seated anger. Now that he was dead I realized just how much I needed to kill him. He was always saying how everything worthless should be done away with. Well, he was a worthless father. I should have done away with him while I had the chance.

But then, I was worthless too. Maybe I should also be dead.

At that moment the ancient alley cat dragged himself up the steps toward me. He could hardly make it. I reached down, picked him up and embraced him. It no longer made any difference that he was filthy and covered with sores.

I scratched his ears and the top of his nose, whispering to him, "You're worthless too, old cat. The only good you are is to keep me company. Now my daddy's dead, I don't need nobody.

"Old cat, would you be my daddy? Maybe if I killed something I could kill off the hate and anger inside me. Be my daddy, old cat. Be . . . my . . . daddy."

He seemed to understand. He stretched out his neck. I scratched him under his chin. A wild purr erupted. I laced my hands around his throat and gave his head a sharp twist. His right claw made two wild, involuntary slashes, scarring me for life at the base of my right thumb and the underside of my wrist. His body went limp as the purr whispered into silence.

Mattie Gringstead called through the torn screen door, "Rog, you come right away. We're carrying yer ma over to the hospital to say good-bye to yer dear dead father before they carry him off to Bunnessen's. It's only right that you should stand by her."

I slipped the body of the old cat beneath the rickety steps and walked into the living room. My mother was sitting in a sagging wing chair, staring straight ahead. There were whispers about her being "made distraught by her grief."

A fussy little man was fluttering from lady to lady in the crowd assembled in response to my mother's initial outcry. It was the ever-distracted Lutheran minister, Pastor Denton Dopplemeyer. Spotting me, he trotted over, his right hand extended. I kept my hand at my side. He grabbed it anyhow and cradled it in his pudgy little palms while assuring me Jesus was shepherding my daddy into a special place of the Spirit resplendent with sapphire streets.

I kept wishing he could find a condoling sentence without an "s." As he pronounced each sibilant, the unwary listener was sprayed with a bit of spit through the gap from a missing upper front tooth.

Releasing my hand, he emitted a high-pitched shriek while waving his palms in the air. At first I thought he'd had a mystic vision and was trying to fly straight into the heavenly realms. Then, I saw that his hands were covered with blood.

I looked down. The deep cat scratches were bleeding profusely into the palm of my hand. Pastor Dopplemeyer executed tiny hops as he howled over and over, "That boy! He bled on me. He bled all over me."

The room was filled with sympathetic babbling. Glares of disapproval were shot in my direction. Once again I was "no damn good." Two matrons escorted the bloody Reverend to the kitchen since it would not be "seemly" for them to accompany him to the bathroom. The sounds of ablutions could be heard from the sink.

I slipped into the forbidden room and washed off the blood. The scratches had closed over. Gritting my teeth, I painted them with iodine.

Entering the living room, I saw Pastor Dopplemeyer had vanished. My appearance was greeted frostily. I stepped to my mother's side and took her hand. Mattie Gringstead rushed forward and removed Mom's hand from mine.

"It's time to go, Mary. You just lean on me. Rog, you follow along now and don't git into any more trouble on the way to my car."

It was dark as we drove to the hospital. I stared at my mother, hardly recognizing the stolid, mask-like set of her face flashing intermittently into view as we passed under streetlights.

We entered Dad's room. It was dark. Through the eastern window I saw the full moon rising. A shaft of its light illumined his face on the white pillow. It resembled the death mask of the mad Napoleon pictured in my history book. I grabbed the sputum pan from his bedside table, rushed to the far corner and vomited again and again.

When nothing more came, I collapsed, quivering on a stern wooden chair. I felt my mother's hand on my shoulder and heard her whisper, "Don't you ever tell all the things he did, boy. Don't you *ever* tell."

Mattie dropped us home. My mother went immediately to bed. I slipped outside and retrieved the body of the old black cat from under the stairs. I wished I could bring him back to life. I found an old rusty shovel in the half-collapsed back shed. I buried him under a lilac bush. Standing there in the moonlight, I promised him I would plant four red tulips over his grave when fall came. I kept my pledge.

Dad's funeral blindsided me. Folk loved the public Frank Robbennolt. He was generous beyond his means and would help anybody who needed an extra pair of hands. After his coffin had been lowered, mourners crowded around me, saying good things:

"Yer sure gonna' miss yer daddy, boy."

"He was the best friend I ever had."

"Best damn oat shocker in Sunrise Township."

"How you musta' loved yer daddy, boy."

I felt a curious interior blow to my emotional solar plexus. It had never occurred to me I was supposed to love my daddy. I hated the abusive tormentor. I was overcome by a guilt I'd never felt before. My daddy made me feel real guilty whenever I did anything wrong, which was just about every day.

This was different. Somewhere in the universe was a love I was supposed to feel for my mindsick daddy. The guilt deepened as the worst thought of all overwhelmed me. If I had found the right way to love him, would he have gotten well? Maybe I really was responsible for my father's angry illness.

Now he was dead. There was no way I could bring him back. I'd even tried to kill him. Maybe I caused the cancer to grow in his lungs because I'd wanted him dead.

The voices around me faded as I stared at his coffin in the bottom of the pit. I was aware that folk were fanning out through the cemetery, visiting the graves of their friends and relatives.

My Hermit Uncle John had appeared for his brother's funeral. He'd carried Mom and me to the service and the graveyard in his antiquated truck. As people faded away after offering final condolences, Mom said to John, "Leave the boy and me alone for a few minutes. We'll join you at the truck."

When we were alone, she said to me, "Roger, I want you to kneel right down here by Frank's grave and make me a promise before yer daddy and God."

I did as she asked. She continued, "I want you to make a solemn sacred promise that you'll never tell as long as you live. You'll never tell what yer daddy did in his darknesses. Make me that promise. Swear me your sacred oath on yer daddy's grave."

My breath came in short gasps. I thought I was going to pass out. I felt like I was hanging naked on the barn wall again when my daddy was trying to teach me not to play.

Her hand descended to my left shoulder. Her fingers were like the talons of a vulture. I was a worthless bit of carrion. I stammered out a promise. I wasn't sure I'd be able to bear the burden the oath laid on me.

A month later we left the farm for good and returned to Pheasant Valley. Mom found a job washing dishes in a greasy spoon cafe. Local prostitutes took their clients to rooms above the establishment. Men would occasionally slip into the kitchen, slap my mother on the butt and invite the Widow Robbennolt upstairs "to know a real man again." She wouldn't respond. She'd continue her stolid task, working her way through mounds of cooking pots and dishes.

One night I stood in a dark alley outside a grease-coated

window, observing her shame as she slapped a marauding male across the face with a hand cracked and bleeding from the harsh detergent. My daddy had been right. I was no damn good. If she didn't have me to worry about, she'd not have to work in this hellhole. The whole world would be better off without me.

I decided to hang myself.

It should be fairly easy. Our house had an empty attic reachable through a trapdoor. Exposed rafters were conveniently located above the opening.

There were two problems: I didn't know how to tie a hangman's noose, and I didn't have a rope.

I remembered that a neighbor who hated me had a length of hemp in his garage. He disliked me because I played the clarinet. It was the one activity which made me feel I was worth something. Some days, I played for four or five hours. The high notes made his dachshund howl. He'd yell across the back fence. I'd keep on playing.

One day, I saw that he was away. I slipped into his garage and "borrowed" the rope he tied behind his boat for summer water skiing. I hid it in our attic.

Next, I went to the public library and checked out *The Complete Encyclopedia of Knots.* I found instructions for tying a hangman's noose.

I fastened the rope securely to a rafter and executed a finely crafted knot. I carried a twenty-five pound bag of flour to the secret place and tested it in the noose. The rope functioned perfectly. I was ready.

I chose a Saturday night when my mother worked late. In the early evening I headed toward the attic. At the last minute I took my teddy bear. He was the only one who would really understand my destructive act — if there was any explanation.

I climbed a kitchen stool and pulled up through the opening, kicking the stool out of the way so I'd not be tempted to save myself on the final drop.

As I made my last-minute preparations, excited sounds emerged from the Methodist Church parking lot up the street.

The roar of tractors, the rattle of hayracks and the shouts of kids heralded a Youth Fellowship outing.

I paused to listen. None of those kids really knew me. They didn't know that one house down from their shouts of joy I was preparing to plummet through a trapdoor. They wouldn't care.

I passed the church every day. Jesus was stuck in their stained glass window. He couldn't get out to help me. The only ones who might come to my rescue were Gletha or John or Tony. There was no way they could be with me. I couldn't see Tony's stars or walk in the woods with Gletha, and my Hermit Uncle John's Mystery in the red fire on Shaman's Point was only a fading memory. In his final months I had allowed my daddy's violence to erase their saving stories.

I removed my clothes. My father had always made me strip before he would hurt me. What I was about to do was the final affirmation of my worthlessness.

I hugged my teddy bear before placing him in the corner. The light fading through the dormer window caressed his single eye. Was it dimmed by a tear?

I checked the knot before dropping it around my neck. As I stepped to the edge of the trapdoor, the parking lot laughter crescendoed. I balanced myself at the opening. I bent my knees. A slight jump would plunge me into oblivion.

Downstairs, I heard the front door creak open. Had my mother gotten off work early? If so, I'd best act quickly. The voice calling up was not hers. It was Hillis Slaymaker, the recently arrived young Methodist minister who lived next door.

"Hey, Rog, are you home?"

Without thinking, I responded with a tentative "Y-Y-Yeah."

"I just wanted to check and see if you're going with us on the hayride?"

I was stunned. He knew my name! He missed *me*. I couldn't remember when I had been missed by anybody — except my daddy when he thought I ought to be someplace I wasn't. There was no way the partygoers would want to wait for a naked kid to get his neck out of a noose and clothes on his body. Since I'd kicked the stool aside, I'd have to drop out of the attic. With my luck I'd probably break my leg.

I stammered out, "I d-d-don't think I'll g-go. I'm not feeling very g-g-good tonight."

Hillis responded, "I'm sorry to hear that. Well, go to bed early and sleep it off. I'll see you in the morning."

The screen door slammed behind the retreating figure.

For three hours I stood on the edge of the trapdoor with the rope around my neck, trying to decide whether or not to carry out my plan. Hillis' caring had triggered memories of other times when I was embraced by hope. The guilt over not having loved my daddy was still terrifying. That's what I was really trying to strangle by the tightening of a noose.

The single voice had stopped me. "He'd see me in the morning"! It would be Sunday. He was assuming I'd be in church.

I listened as the revelers returned from their country outing. Silence descended. I stepped back from the opening.

I removed the noose from my neck and coiled it carefully in the corner. The bear looked relieved.

I left the rope there for six months, waiting to be fully certain that somebody really cared for me. If I wasn't convinced, I could always use it.

I dropped my clothes and my bear through the opening. I got a firm grip on its edges and swung myself to the floor without incident. I grabbed the trapdoor's dangling cord and slammed it shut. The sound echoed through the silent house — a tympani beat of hope.

I followed Hillis' orders and went to bed. Before falling into a dreamless sleep a single thought occurred to me: Perhaps, for a moment, Jesus *had* stepped out of the stained glass window and saved me.

The Seashore

Dawn light seeped into the shack. The old heron was outlined in the window. I stumbled to my feet, grabbed a couple of shrimp and pushed open the glass panel. Without thinking, I queried, "Hey, Tony! Have you been here all night?"

At the sound of my naming, the heron's head snapped around, and he stared at me for a long moment without touching the shrimp. He tilted his beak toward the morning sky and emitted a soft, lonely cry. He daintily accepted the offering in my palm. In the ear of my heart I heard a prayer uttered by the old Lakota shaman, Tony Great Turtle, to Mother Earth, seeking forgiveness for consuming her children in order to sustain his life.

The great bird spread his gigantic wings and glided high out over the glistening sea.

I bent wearily over the battered table and hit the "print" mode. The first two tales began clattering out of the elderly machine. I needed hard copy for later sharing with Blind Ben and Rose.

Straightening up, I surveyed my strange abode: a cot, a crucifix, a bear and a computer. I had inadvertently shaped for myself a hermitage, a monk's cell in which I was copying a manuscript from my wounded heart.

I felt no hunger. I stepped to the rusted sink and drank a tin cup of water. Perhaps I could go all the way and fast through the process of clearing out the memories.

I needed sleep. The clock registered 6:30 A.M. Pulling the frayed twine and extinguishing the twenty-five watts of light, I stretched out on the cot. The computer screen illumined the crucifix and bear like a bizarre votive candle. The printer's rhythmic clatter was a soothing chant celebrating my release.

The last thing I remembered was the smile of Christ emanating from between his welcoming arms.

I was awakened, fully alert, by the strident sound of a car horn. The clock registered 5 P.M. My critics and confidants awaited me. I formally attired myself for the occasion. Pulling on my Speedo, I slipped into faded denim cutoffs and a ragged tee shirt emblazoned with a daisy and the words "Make love, not war."

I tore off the manuscript which lay in a folded pile by the printer and headed for the chariot which would carry me to the beachside confessional.

Following barely discernible ruts in the sand, we arrived at our isolated refuge. I opened Ben's door. He blindly searched for a guiding arm. He tottered for a moment and nearly fell. I half-carried him to his fading gilded throne. Ramblin' Rose followed protectively, carrying the buffalo robe.

We settled Ben in his chair and covered his legs. He removed his ever-present dark glasses. The shattered sockets had healed a bit over the years. I wondered if his shame had resolved itself. He'd been caught by a jealous husband who threw acid in the face of his wife's lover, who was also the preacher at the local Baptist church. The late afternoon sun reflected burnished gold in sockets where once eyes had glowed.

As Rose and I settled in the sand at his feet, I glanced up. He seemed to be sensing the far horizon. I knew that he, like the blind poet Homer, was in touch with an inner sight which brought alive the wine-dark sea.

Ben asked, "Is my old friend, the heron, wading at the ocean's edge?"

Rose assured him that he was.

I said, "Ben, though this is therapy for me, these tales are really gifts. You were a saving presence when I was sixteen."

Rose interrupted wryly, "I suppose they'll be pure entertainment for me."

Ben broke in imperiously, "Just stop palavering and read,

boy. Read!"

For the next two hours I read "Enter Sharee" and "The Fist, the Rifle, the Rape, the Rope." Darkness fell. I improvised the last few pages.

As I drew to a close, Rose's arms encircled me. Ben's hands found the top of my head. No words were spoken. Ben massaged my scalp lightly. I felt a kind of ordination from the flawed old holy man to continue my healing journey.

We folded the robe and returned to the car along a moonlit path.

When they dropped me off near the shack, Rose queried quietly, "Tomorrow?"

I responded, "Tomorrow."

Ben halted my exit with a question: "Boy, if you let your anger tear at your gut, destroying you and others you terrorize with your tongue, your mindsick daddy wins. Do you want your mindsick daddy to win?"

I whispered, "No."

The lights from the dash illumined the wry grin spreading over his face. Removing his glasses, he continued, "Then write, boy. Write!"

Rose reached under the driver's seat and handed me a package wrapped in Sunday comics. I took it without a word. They drove off. I watched their headlights bounce over the rutted trail looking like the eyes of a retreating dragon. I let emotion from the night's reading disappear with their lights.

I entered the sanctuary. I pulled on the dangling light and opened the package. There lay a golden shirt like the one I wore as part of Blind Ben See's Carnival of Wonders. The logo eye on the pocket glowed more brightly than the dim bulb above my head.

The great heron peered through the window. His mystic eye matched the one on the shirt as I hung it over the milk-crate bureau.

The bear and the Christ welcomed me home.

I stripped off my clothes in preparation for a quick swim. I changed my mind. Words were crying out to be written. I sat at the computer and let them flow.

Paradise Gained

My reverie, called forth by the full moon in the mural on Sharee's van, was broken by a sharp slap on the butt and the raucous voice of Skip Arrowsmith. Skip was a senior and quarterback of the Pheasant Valley High School football team, the Bird Dogs. As he strutted around town, he always had a pigskin securely cradled in his left armpit, giving the impression it had been there since birth. He was ever shadowed by Tiny Feldman, his wide receiver.

Skip placed a patronizing arm around my shoulder and hissed, "Hey, Rog, Tiny and me have been watching you from the park. You've been staring at those pictures of near-naked ladies for about ten minutes. If you were a real man, you'd find yourself one in the flesh. I bet we could fix you up with a babe who would put out, no questions asked."

In the eyes of most of the boys around town, Skip was a real man. Not only was he a star on the field, but he'd gotten Jennie Towner, the lead cheerleader, pregnant. She'd just come back after a long "visit with her aunt." Everybody knew where she'd really been. I guessed she'd given the baby up for adoption. I hoped it fared better than I had.

My face was burning with shame at being discovered. I mumbled, "I gotta' get back to the store."

The boys hooted with laughter. I heard Skip command his shadow, "Okay, Tiny. C-l-e-a-r across the park for a long one!"

I marveled as the high-arching ball thudded into unfailing hands.

A master plan whisked into my mind. I could find Blind Ben See's Carnival of Wonders. It had played the vacant lot near the sign of the Flying Red Horse gas station just last week.

I'd join the troupe. That would provide me with two advantages. I'd be near her — the beautiful apparition I'd accompanied from the grocery store, and I would leave Pheasant Valley, hopefully forever.

It shouldn't be too difficult. Mom had gone north to Bear Run Township. She was helping to care for my weakening Aunt Jennie Maulden. I was to keep in touch with her by phone twice a week. I could do that from anywhere. I would tell two or three people in Pheasant Valley who might be concerned that Aunt Jennie was reaching the end of her life and was calling for me to be at her death bed. Weaving a web of lies freed me to disappear.

And disappear I did.

It was Saturday night. I shared with Axel that I had a "family emergency." He expressed condolences over the condition of my aunt and hoped I would be back real soon. Then he spoke magic words: "Boy, yer just about the best worker I've ever had."

He stepped to the cash register till and handed me $27.50 for fifty hours of work. He paused for a moment, scratching the wart on his neck. He reached into the till a second time and handed me two one dollar bills and two quarters, saying, "I'm gonna' round it off to thirty dollars in case yuh need a little extry fer yer trip. Yuh git yerself back here jist as fast as yuh can."

I lifted my chin and squared my shoulders. Sharee had called me a man. Axel said I worked good. The words triggered feelings of worth engendered by Gletha, John and Tony. The gnawing guilt over never loving my daddy receded. I marched hopefully out of the store with cadences of "Under the Double Eagle" — which we'd played last year in the marching band — echoing in my heart.

I stepped briskly down the street, pausing momentarily to glance behind me. Axel was turning out the lights. As the Red Owl on the sign stared back at me, the fluorescent tubing began to dim. He winked at me. Then all was dark.

I didn't have a suitcase. I stopped behind the liquor store and picked up a heavy cardboard box emblazoned with **OLD CROW WHISKEY** from which to craft a case for my few belongings. The words on the box made me feel grown-up and worldly. I had to feel a lot of that if I expected to succeed in life with the carnival.

I rushed home. My first task was to rig rope around my box so I had a handle to carry it by. For a second time in my life I had no rope when I needed it. Then, I remembered: the coil with which I'd planned to hang myself was still in the corner of the attic.

I headed upstairs, carrying the kitchen stool and a flashlight. I climbed into the dark. The rope gleamed invitingly in the beam of light. All the old memories shot through my mind. I quickly grabbed the twisted hemp and dropped through the opening to the waiting stool. The possibility of killing myself had blindsided me in that fear-filled little cavern. I fully realized for the first time that I would always walk an emotional tightrope.

Returning to the box, I took a butcher knife and carved two holes in the side through which to string a handle. I threw in an extra pair of bib overalls, two faded shirts, socks and underwear. After my daddy died, Mom again sewed me boxer shorts from flour sacks with the logo of the girl and her dog ever on the rear.

I glanced around the tiny room with its peeling wallpaper. I wondered if I'd be back. My breath caught as I spotted my teddy bear enthroned on a pillow case embroidered with hollyhocks. He was staring at me bleakly through his single button eye.

I knelt by the side of my bed and cradled him against my cheek. All of a sudden I wasn't feeling quite so much like a man. I was torn. Would a real man carry a stuffed bear on what he hoped would be the greatest adventure of his life?

Since I had a problem feeling consistently real, I gently packed the bear next to the girl and her dog and headed downstairs.

I securely tied my makeshift case with the heavy cord. The handle loop worked well.

My mother was always "tying up loose ends." I had one more bit of guilt to deal with. Most of the stolen hemp from my angry neighbor's garage lay on the kitchen floor. My inherent sense of honesty said I should return it.

I picked up the rope and stepped into our backyard. The stars stared down like God's unrelenting eyes. I had to do it.

There were no visible house lights. Hopefully, everyone was asleep. I crept across the yard, flashlight in hand and entered the cavernous garage. I spotted the hook and reached up to return the stolen property.

Lights blazed! I spun guiltily around and found myself staring into the barrel of a shotgun. My gigantic neighbor exploded, "You dirty little worthless sneak thief! What the hell are you doing in my garage at one-thirty in the morning?"

My stammer, which I was working on with the help of a teacher at school, returned in spades, "I-I-I had j-j-just b-b-borrowed it. I g-g-got c-c-called out of t-t-town and th-th-thought I had b-b-better return it b-b-before I left."

"'Borrowed' it? That's a damned lie. I bin lookin' fer that cord fer a year. I hadda' buy me a new one. Yuh barefaced stole it. So yuh decided to put it back and steal somethin' better, eh? I oughta' pepper yuh with birdshot. Now, yuh git yer butt outta here, yuh no-good little sonofabitch. Yer gonna' end up in reform school or with somebody pluggin' yuh between the eyes. Believe me, the world would be better off with yuh dead so's nobody'd hafta' put up with yer stupid noise and yer thievin' ways."

Echoes of my daddy's voice rang out. I crept out of the gun's range, feeling, as my Aunt Jennie used to say, "lower than a snake's belly."

As I slithered across the dew-soaked lawn with the neighbor's eyes boring into my back, I once again questioned everything about myself. It was probably the dumbest thing I'd ever done in my life to even think about following Sharee into the carnival. She'd laugh at my infatuation. I wouldn't be able to get a job. My thirty dollars would not last forever. They could display me in the freak show along with the Crocodile Kid and the World's Smallest Pony. They'd hang me by the wrists against a black backdrop and flash a neon sign which read, "The Boy with a Hole in His Heart."

I wished my bear wasn't packed. I needed a little skin-to-fur comfort. I picked up my carton of belongings, locked the house and headed for Highway 14, hoping for a lift from an all-night trucker.

I headed west. I trudged through the moonless night amazed at the breathtaking brilliance of the stars. One fell in the distance. I remembered Tony Great Turtle telling me how falling stars were really figures of celestial evil — "dark star people" he had defeated on his vision quest. I hoped the star would bring me luck.

It did. The descending light merged with the distant flash of headlights. I hoped the accompanying roar signified a cross-country hauler who was lonesome in the wee hours of the morning.

I stood in the roadway as long as I dared till the beam of his brights hit me. I jumped to the side and waved. The gigantic vehicle passed me. It slowed to a stop far down the road. I ran as fast as I could. The makeshift case thudded against my right leg.

As I got nearer, a voice called out, "No need to hurry, boy. I got a little business to attend to."

The man had left the truck and relieved himself in the ditch. I stayed back a respectful distance. When I saw him disappear around the front, I walked alongside. The door on the passenger side was open. I climbed in.

Light from the dash illumined the printing on the carton in my lap. He burst into a hearty guffaw and exploded, "Well, kid, I hope that box contains what it says it does. We can stop in a roadside park about twenty miles ahead and have ourselves a little party. I'm always glad to have a knight of the road well prepared for his wanderings."

I sorrily confessed, "The box only contains my clothes and my . . . ."

I almost said "teddy bear." I caught myself in time. A knight of the road would not be carrying a stuffed animal.

The driver queried, "Where you headed?"

"Maple River."

"Why would anybody be goin' tuh Maple River? I broke down once a few miles out. Ain't much there."

I told him that I was going to get a job in a carnival. He smiled thoughtfully but made no comment. He changed the subject: "Well, kid, you got a tough job for the next three hours until we git to yer destination. I was feelin' mighty tired. I tried talkin' to myself, but I damn near bored me to sleep. Just listen to me talk. Talk back. Don't you dare fall asleep. If all goes well, we'll make it through till daylight."

We made it through till daylight. During the wee hours of the morning he regaled me with tales of near freezing to death in blizzards and near frying in deserts and of front tires blowing, sending rigs hurtling down cliffs. The narration was underscored by the growl of the gigantic engine. I was scared to death. It was better than listening to "The Shadow" on the radio. I certainly had no trouble staying awake.

The sun was just appearing over the horizon in the rearview mirror when he dropped me at the edge of Maple River. He was heading for Sioux Falls, South Dakota. I almost changed my plans and stayed with him to hear more of his endless tales.

In the distance, I could just make out the tip of the Star of Bethlehem Ferris wheel. It appeared the planet Venus was resting in the topmost seat before fleeing the rising sun. I said good-bye and watched the great beast of a truck lumber on down the highway.

I headed for the carnival grounds to continue my quest.

I trudged two miles toward the dusty lot, shifting my carrying case from cramped hand to cramped hand.

I had a strategy in mind. For the past two years when Blind Ben's carnival came to Pheasant Valley, I picked up a couple of bucks a night after Axel's store closed by washing dishes for Hamburger Jack, who ran a one-man food service at the carnival. When the crowds got heavy, he needed a little extra help. One time I was passing down the Midway as Jack was desperately trying to wash his battered plates while flipping burgers. He caught my eye and called, "Hey, kid! C'mere and give me a hand. I'll make it worth your while."

When things quieted down a bit, he commented, "You have an honest look about you, and you work real good. I wish I could take you with me on the road."

Now I could offer him that golden opportunity. I'd chosen my destination for the night's odyssey from a comment he'd made: "Wish I could take you on with me to Maple River. We get a coupla' days off and then play a week's run."

By the time I arrived at the lot, the roustabouts and game operators were coming out of the cook tent. The enterprise was swinging into life. Townspeople were already lining up to buy tickets for the rides and wandering around the perimeter of the tents, hoping to get a free glimpse of The World's Fattest Woman on the way to her sideshow.

Jack's miniature dining tent was at the entrance to the Midway. I followed my nose. His offering was distinguished by mixing a bit of basil with the meat. He said it drew folk like flies to his table rather than satisfying their hunger at one of the fifteen other food booths. He also surreptitiously added a generous amount of cooked oatmeal to "extend the product." As a seasoned thumb-weigher, I appreciated his skill at culinary subterfuge, even if I did have an "honest look" about me.

I stepped up to the serving counter. He turned, spotted me and exploded, "Rog! What are you doing here? You're a sight for sore eyes. C'mere and let me give you a hug."

He reached his great hairy arms over the counter and pulled me to his barrel chest. It felt good. Jack carried at least two hundred and fifty pounds on his six foot frame. He'd been a dock worker in San Francisco until his wife and twelve-year-old son were killed in an apartment fire. He'd hit the road trying to outrun his grief. He ended up operating a food concession for Blind Ben. He'd told me I reminded him of his boy.

I hoped Jack might adopt me. He'd make a great second daddy.

Releasing me reluctantly, he queried, "What can I do for you, kid?"

I was tempted to tell him about the beautiful magnet which had drawn me to the traveling gala. However, I simply responded, "I had to get away from Pheasant Valley for awhile. I was hoping you'd give me a job."

His face clouded. "I can pick up temporary help as we go along. Any permanent jobs are handled by Blind Ben See. Tell you what you should do, kid. Go over to the Fun House. This would be a good time since the show is not quite open yet. He always oversees our operation from the platform. He may be blind, but he doesn't miss a thing. He's got second sight. He seems to see everything inside himself.

"Now listen, kid. You know I like you a lot. Let me clue you in, though Ben has sworn us all to silence on this point. You know the story — how he was a Baptist preacher man. He was playing around with a woman in his church, and her husband caught them together and threw some kind of acid in his face. It burned out his eyes. That's why he always wears those dark glasses.

"I'll let you in on a little secret. Whenever he interviews anybody for a job, midway through their talk, he slips off his glasses. If a person gasps at the ugly sight of maturating pits in the middle of his face with acid burn scars all around, Ben refuses to hire 'em. He always says if you can't confront the terror of his face with serenity, you have no business in a carnival — or probably anyplace else for that matter. You've got to always see the person behind the terror.

"So, go and talk to him. I heard there weren't no jobs on the lot. But you never know from day to day. Come on back and I'll give you a burger before I add the oatmeal. Good luck, kid."

He slapped me on the back with a force that took my breath away. I thanked him and headed for the Fun House.

The concessionaires were in their places, hoping to collect a few bucks from early arrivals. I loved their spiels. A gawky, pimply faced kid about my age with an emaciated, pale-faced girl on his arm strolled slowly by the Marksmanship Booth with its continuous row of battered tin animals passing on a conveyor across the back of the small tent. The operator leaned over the counter and spoke in reassuring tones: "Hey, young man. Step over here for a minute."

The couple paused. That was their first mistake.

He continued, "You look like you've done a fair amount of hunting. Why doncha' step right up to this here counter and pop off three of those beasts back there. Win a giant panda for that b-e-e-yoot-iful creature on yer arm."

Her eyes were glued to a huge, dusty stuffed panda dangling in the midst of a hundred far lesser prizes.

The boy strutted to the counter, carelessly picked up a pop gun and began firing away. The rolling targets remained unscathed. His aim may have been skewed by the fact that his companion refused to remove her hand from his arm.

The morning air was shattered by the sound of his repeated firing. Ten minutes later and two bucks poorer, he stumbled sheepishly away. Her face was a mask of disappointment.

Another youth swaggered to the counter, his shirt open to his naval, a pack of Chesterfield cigarettes rolled into its short sleeve. He carelessly threw down some coins and picked up the gun. His first three shots eliminated a squirrel, a rabbit and a deer whose tin antlers were shapelessly twisted.

The operator reached reluctantly for the giant prize. The champion curled his left arm around the panda and turned to leer at the girl who had paused to observe his performance. He casually unbuttoned the final button above his studded belt, revealing the beginnings of dark hair cascading up from his hidden places.

She shuddered involuntarily. Her companion grabbed her arm and dragged her roughly away. She kept surreptitiously glancing over her shoulder as she was towed down the Midway. The jeering laughter of the triumphant marksman followed them.

I walked toward the recorded sounds of shrieks and roars emanating from the Fun House. They were counterpointed by the sharp thuds of baseballs hitting canvas.

I rounded a corner and saw a young man in a gold shirt hurling baseballs at carefully weighted concrete "milk bottles" pyramided on a small platform twenty feet from the counter. All carnival workers wore bright gold shirts with a black eye outlined on the pockets to distinguish them from the crowd. If there was any trouble, the perpetrators found themselves immediately surrounded.

The baseball player's right arm was missing clear to his shoulderblade. With each infuriated left-handed throw he would pick off a single bottle. He must have felt me staring in dumb amazement at his skill. He turned. His face was a mask of anger. He ground out, "Well, don't just stand there gawking. Either buy some balls and knock 'em over for yourself or be on about your business."

I shamefacedly hurried away. I had violated something. I wasn't sure what.

The Fun House loomed ahead. Gilded monsters with gaping jaws framed the attraction. Customers entered through a giant death's head. Across the back were the great Mirrors of Truth, which shot the image of passersby ten feet tall or crumpled them into fat balls.

A spare figure was sitting in his great chipped golden chair, a dark slouch hat protecting his balding head, the morning light glinting off heavy dark glasses. He wore a gold shirt and red tie beneath his shiny three-piece black suit. It was Blind Ben See himself.

I'd met him once before when he'd come to my Hermit Uncle John's with Tony Great Turtle. I hoped he might remember me. The early patrons had not made it as far into the show grounds as the Fun House. He was surveying his domain and recording on his inner screen everything happening around him through smells and sounds and movement.

I screwed up my courage. Before I could step up on the platform, he spoke: "At least you're not limping this time."

I was flabbergasted. How could the blind man know that I

was the kid he'd helped Tony Great Turtle and my Hermit Uncle John turn into a *hunka*, a beloved one, on Shaman's Point above Lake Sumac four years ago after my daddy had hurt my leg?

"I'm not limping outside. But I'm still kinda' limping inside. I need work real bad. Your show played Pheasant Valley a few days ago. I helped Hamburger Jack. I thought maybe I could get a job somewhere in the carnival."

He was silent for a moment and then queried quietly, "Is your daddy still hurting you?"

"My daddy's dead. But sometimes even the memory of what he did hurts me real bad."

Ben's voice was almost a whisper: "Memories of terror can sometimes whip you almost to death. You've got to stack up enough saving memories to balance them off and keep you hopeful so as to go on living. I think you probably need to work in my carnival for awhile."

My heart turned a flip-flop of joy. Before I could babble out my thanks, his left hand moved casually toward his face. He removed his dark glasses. The empty pits where his eyes had been resembled the runny sores on the back of the old black cat I had killed in place of my father. There was no need to gasp.

He returned his glasses to his nose and asked, "How old are you, young man?"

I thought quickly. I knew the law. I couldn't work in a place like this until I was eighteen. Again, I sacrificed a lie for a job and responded, "I'm eighteen, sir."

He thought for a moment, "I don't know what kind of math they're teaching in schools these days, but the more I think about it, you can't be much beyond sixteen. How tall are you?"

"I'm almost six-foot-three."

"Let me feel your face."

I was embarrassed. I hadn't shaved for two days. He passed his hand over the fine stubble. His touch was incredibly gentle as he commented, "You're shaving and you're tall. A carnival is a place of make-believe, so we'll just make believe you're eighteen. I've noticed one thing changed about you. There's hardly any stammer when you talk. What happened?"

I almost tripped over words as I replied, "My high school English teacher discovered that if I memorized stuff I didn't stammer when I recited it. I've been acting in a lot of plays. I've discovered if I wander around pretending I'm on stage all the time I can talk clearly."

Ben chuckled, "You'll do fine in a carnival. Nobody's here unless they're trying to act out their lives beyond something in their past. Your voice sounds good. How long do you think you could talk without stopping?"

I was puzzled by his question. "When I get a part in a play, I'll go off by myself and shout out my lines for hours to make sure I won't ever stammer them."

I was feeling confident and was about to rehearse for him my various dramatic triumphs when he interrupted, "You'll do fine, Rog. I even remembered your name after four years. Not bad for an old blind man. There's only one job open on the lot. We've just been joined by a new girlie show. They need a spieler. You walk on down the Midway until you find the van labeled 'Ze Bra.' The lead dancer's named Sharee. She's waiting for two more girls to join her tomorrow when we hit Foxton. She can work with you today and teach you the calls. You can start tomorrow afternoon."

He concluded with rough gentleness, "Now get your butt off this platform. I've got work to do."

He must have heard the dazed celebration rollicking inside me. He added, "One caution, young man. Don't you even think about touching a woman in any show of mine. In this exhibition, we've all had so much pain that we're a family. There's no way we're going to risk destroying one another that way."

I mumbled my thanks and descended. The Mirrors of Truth levitated my image high above the Midway. I was going to work with the most beautiful woman in the world. She had called me a man.

I headed for paradise in a jungle glen.

Seashore

As I finished the story, the old heron outside the window flapped his wings as if applauding.

I was experiencing a deep-running joy. I could not stop now. Without a glance at the clock, I began the next tale.

Two Transformations

I picked up my box and crossed the Midway to share my good fortune with Hamburger Jack. I paused to watch the ball hurler systematically pick off bottle after bottle. He'd alternate between cleanly collapsing the entire setup with one ball and neatly demolishing the structure one unit at a time.

A crowd gathered to scrutinize his skill. The more people observing, the harder he threw. I expected a ball to penetrate the canvas at any moment. His flowing rhythm was amazing.

There were three stacks so that three customers might simultaneously try their luck. He'd alternate his technique stack by stack, reset and repeat. Finally he'd turn and wordlessly offer a handful of balls to a gaping onlooker. Having witnessed the ease of his performance, players quickly lined up in three neat queues to try their luck. Most retreated without the longed-for Kewpie doll or teddy bear.

When one group of disappointed onlookers turned away, he resumed his solitary throwing. Something sketched on the canvas behind the center bottle column caught my eye. It was a rough outline of what, at first glance, appeared to be a death's head. The empty sockets stared at me blankly. Then I noticed that the artist had added a unique feature: a long flowing mustache. In my imagination I added a full moon. My vision was shattered by the center stack of bottles exploding into the face.

The thrower paused in his ritual and stared at me. Pain met

pain. I hurried on.

Hamburger Jack rejoiced at my good fortune. He turned the gas off under his great pot of burbling oatmeal and walked me over to the administration van where I was introduced to Grandma Nell who kept the books and generally assisted Blind Ben. She spent a few hours a day playing the merry-go-round calliope. She greeted me warmly and handed me two dark gold shirts. I'd have performance clothes, but when I was offstage, I should always wear the special shirt so everybody would know I was "part of the family." Her words were music to my ears.

A large open eye was embroidered on each shirt pocket. Carnival folk are a superstitious lot. It was a widely held opinion that these eyes were mysteriously connected to Blind Ben. Wherever a wearer moved, Ben could "see" on his interior mindscreen everything within the purview of the eye. A perpetual pinochle player would be dumbfounded when Ben commented, "You sure did win big last night" under conditions where the player felt it would be impossible for him to know by any means other than his strange clairvoyance.

Jack paused at his van and invited me to step in and change my shirt. The little travel trailer seemed much too small for the giant man. He remained outside and called to me, "It's real cozy in there. I haven't got much that I really need so I just curl myself up and I'm fine. Tell you what, boy. I've got an extra blanket. You can sleep in the seat of my old Dodge truck until you get yourself squared away."

I thanked him, stowed my box and headed toward paradise in a traveling jungle glen.

Sharee had folded out a little stage which was backed by the painting on the side of the van. As I walked up, she was on her knees washing off a dusty artificial palm down stage left. In the soft morning light I thought she looked like a mangerside Madonna.

She turned and saw me coming. Her brow furrowed as she tried to remember where she'd laid eyes on me. She rose quickly and came to the edge of the stage. Her low, husky voice shaped words of welcome: "I know you. You're the nice young man who carried my groceries for me in some little burg a day or two ago."

I interrupted, "It was Pheasant Valley."

She continued, "Yes, that's probably where it was. You also waited on me when the old biddy at the counter called me a floozy."

"That was Selma. She's a hellfire and damnation Baptist who's got herself some pretty strong ideas about what's right and wrong."

Sharee stared off into the distance, watching the morning light glance off the steel mirrors mounted on the Star of Bethlehem Ferris wheel. She commented softly, "There must be a whole lot of Bibles out there missing a line that I've read in mine: 'Judge not that ye be not judged.'"

She broke her brief reverie and turned back to me. "What are you doing here with that shirt on?"

I responded, "Blind Ben gave me a job. He said I was to report to you. I'm to be your new s-s-s-"

The old stammering ghost was coming back to haunt me. I took a deep breath, pretended I was onstage — which I hoped I'd soon be — and clearly enunciated the final word: "spieler."

There was a slight intake of breath from the stage: "You — our spieler?"

She looked me up and down. There was nothing I could do to hide the faded bib overalls and worn high-top work shoes.

She mused, "We're going to have to effect a major transformation. You can't walk out on my stage dressed like that."

I panicked. I had an instantaneous vision of myself entering together with ladies like those dancing in the moonlight behind me — nude except for a minuscule scrap of zebra-striped fabric wrapped around my essentials.

Sharee continued, "You come back at noon, Rog. I passed an S & L Department Store on the way to the lot. They'll have some clothes that'll be a little more appropriate for a spieler on a cooch show platform."

Worry descended. My dad had a niece, Henrietta, who lived in Maple River. She was head cashier in the S & L. This involved sitting in a small cubicle high above the store from which cables extended downward to stations where clerks waited on customers. A shopper would hand the clerk money for a purchase. The cash and sales slip would be placed in a little cup fastened to the cable. A cord would be pulled as the cup whizzed upward to the delight of small children who paused in their games of hide-and-seek amidst the dangling dry goods and watched the glimmering cups dance above their heads. In a moment the carriers would return to their source bearing change and the sales slip marked "paid" or "charged."

The ceiling of the store was crafted from molded metal panels embossed with vines. On a busy day the crisscrossing conveyors and their buzzing passage resembled a madcap ballet of giant bumblebees.

From her vantage point Henrietta could see everything and everybody who happened into the store. She knew who was visiting from out of town because the S & L was a major stop if you were "showing the city" to outsiders. This made her the ideal scribe for the "Know Your Neighbors" column of the Maple River Weekly Tribune.

She was privy to intimate details such as the corset sizes of every lady in the hamlet. At Saturday night card club someone would query, "I wonder if Bertie Bartlesen hasn't lost a little weight lately."

Henrietta would knowingly reply, "Not in the last seven years."

She would most certainly see me in the store with Sharee. I hadn't the faintest idea how I might explain. Not only would the entire family be informed that Rog had disgraced them all by being seen in public with a "painted lady" but the incident would probably be reported in the Tribune on the following Friday.

We'd visited her a time or two. She had once taken us for lunch at the locally famous Barleybeard Cafe. The proprietress, Mitzie Mitchelson, prided herself on her house special: a grilled bologna sandwich on whole wheat, sided by a generous dollop of her blue-ribbon potato salad. Every year Mitzie packed lunches for the county fair judges, "as a public service." Every year a blue-ribbon appeared on her salad.

The ribbons were proudly mounted on the glass of the pie case. There were so many you could hardly see what had been fresh-baked for the day, though the regulars knew it was probably apple and cherry since Mitzie didn't like to "fuss around with creams and meringues." She preferred to "toss a little fruit into the richest pie crust in town." She always added an enormous roll of thumb-creased pastry around the edge of the pan. Most customers would carefully break this off their serving and dunk it in their milk or coffee. It was like having two desserts.

As I left Sharee, a plan to avoid detection shaped itself in my mind. I would call Henrietta and offer to meet her for lunch at the Barleybeard. If I didn't show, she'd stay on and have the special and grill Mitzie on any gossip for her column.

The plan worked perfectly. I made the call. Henrietta was touched beyond measure. I concocted a now-forgotten cock-and-bull story about how I happened to be in town.

Sharee and I arrived at the store. My unsuspecting cousin was nowhere in sight. We headed for the Men's Department. Sharee knew exactly what she was looking for. She asked the gaping young clerk to run a tape measure over me so whatever we bought would fit perfectly. He had a little trouble removing his eyes from her perfect attributes to do as she requested. He was obviously longing to run a tape measure over her.

She quickly chose two pairs of tight black pants, two white shirts made of soft flowing fabric with long full sleeves, a pair of the shiniest black shoes I'd ever seen in my life and two pairs of black socks. She said, "Step behind that changing curtain and try on a set of these."

I did as she requested. I shucked off my overalls, my gold shirt and my scarred shoes. I stared at the tall, wan, skinny, sad-eyed figure in the mirror. I wished I could remove the boxer shorts which my mother made from flour sacks. I hated the child and her dog in the logo on the seat.

I slipped into my new apparel. I turned and looked into the mirror. I didn't recognize the magnificent figure who stared back. The man in the mirror straightened his shoulders. A confident gleam came into his eyes. A smile curved at the corners of his mouth. It took me a while to realize it was me.

I stepped through the curtain. A low whispered "w-o-w" escaped from the clerk's lips. Sharee looked at me appreciatively for a moment, then stepped forward and unbuttoned my shirt to just above my naval. She stepped back and commented, "Rog, I think I've just transformed you into a cooch show caller."

I could see the clerk was about to die from envy.

While I'd been changing, Sharee had picked up two pairs of dark green work pants which would look real nice with my gold shirts. I took a pair of the pants with me and headed for the changing curtain. On my way I paused at the underwear table. I picked up two pairs of briefs — and a jockstrap to wear with my costume. Now I could wear the strap not as a sign of my daddy's punishment but of my pride in myself.

I changed into the new briefs and work pants. I left the bib overalls and flour sack boxers in a crumpled heap on the floor.

I emerged and took another look in the long mirror. A confident, grinning carney was framed in heavy walnut. The eye on my pocket winked back.

Sharee paid for the purchases, saying that the cost would be deducted from my first check. I heaved a sigh of relief. I hadn't had to touch my thirty dollars from Axel.

We left the store. I floated at her side, a free man.

We reached the lot and headed for the cook tent. The sound of laughter and the rich smell of beef stew overcame me. I was both heart-starved and belly-starved. We stepped through the flap. Twenty folding tables with eight roustabouts and performers at each were crowded into the tent.

Grandma Nell called to Sharee, "Get your food and come on over. We've got some business to talk through."

The only empty seat under the canvas covering was at Nell's side. Sharee left me on my own. I wanted to bolt, but sheer hunger overcame me. I stepped to the serving counter and picked up a worn tray and battered silverware.

A smiling lady in a spattered apron put a generous bowl of

stew on my tray, added three huge biscuits and a side of peach cobbler. She spoke: "Yer new, aint'cha? My name's Ramblin' Rose."

Her words emerged from a twisted mouth which stood at the center of an ugly scar traversing her face from just below her left ear and disappearing into the soft folds of fat in the center of her throat. I couldn't help staring open-mouthed at her terrible disfigurement.

She continued matter-of-factly, "Close your mouth, boy. Your heart will get cold. Take a good look at my little beauty mark now. Next time you come through you won't have to bother with it. My man came home drunker than usual one day and decided he didn't want me around. He did a little artwork with his knife. I damn near bled to death.

"They threw him in jail until I healed. I hooked up with Ben's show, and I've bin runnin' ever since. That was twenty-eight years ago.

"Let me tell you somethin', kid, that might help you understand yer new family. Everybody here is scarred one way or another. When we talk among ourselves, we call this the Scartown Show instead of our official title: Blind Ben See's Carnival of Wonders. If a person thinks they're perfect, they won't last long around here."

I responded, "I'll fit in just fine. I'm sorry I stared at your scar, but it does stand out real good. I'm Rog. I'm new, and I'm glad to see some food, since I haven't managed to eat in quite awhile."

A look of concern washed over her face, obliterating the scar. She said, "You jist hand me back yer tray."

I did as I was told. She put in another ladle of stew which brought the steaming victuals nearly to overflow. She added a fourth biscuit and nestled the bowl neatly in their midst to soak up any gravy I might spill. She handed back the tray with a conspiratorial wink.

I searched the tent for a place to sit. There were no empty spaces. I headed for the exit but was stopped by a light tug on my pant leg. I looked down and saw the tiniest girl I'd ever seen. She stared up at me as if she were contemplating scaling a mountain. Her high, thin voice was barely audible above the surrounding hubbub.

"If you don't mind kneeling, you can put your food on the end of our table."

I thanked her. She couldn't reach my hand but guided me through the crowd by holding on to my left pant leg just below the knee.

In a far corner of the tent was a low table surrounded by little people. I'd never been this close to dwarves before. Two of them reached up and lowered my tray to the faded red-checked oilcloth. I knelt awkwardly on the crushed grass.

The man on my left said, "You've just become an honorary member of Oscar Sidelka's Greatest Little Show on Earth. We do acrobatics and a Tom Thumb Wedding. I'm Oscar."

I responded, "I'm Rog. I'm the new spieler over at Ze Bra."

Oscar's face clouded for a moment as he spoke: "Everybody's got to make a living some way. That just would never be my way."

I shivered. I had just been judged by a miniature prophet. I picked up my spoon to eat but was stopped by the minuscule child who clung to my side: "You can't eat food without praying over it. Maybe you don't know how. I'll be glad to do it for you."

I bowed my head. She began to rhythmically clap her tiny hands and chant,

Bless this food,
Bless this man,
Present One
Since the world began.
Amen.

Tears flowed down my cheeks. Echoes of Gletha's forest prayers and Tony Great Turtle's saving ceremonies were woven together with the soul-touching doggerel of the tiny girl. Once again I'd found an unexpected place of refuge.

A miniature hand stroked the back of mine. I opened my eyes. It was Oscar. He said softly, "It's always a good thing to wash out our hearts. I'm glad Rix's prayer turned on the faucet of your soul."

I wiped my eyes on the rough paper napkin Ramblin' Rose had put on my tray. I looked down at the source of the prayer who had drawn her chair close to mine and queried, "I don't think I've ever met anybody named Rix before."

A chorus of gentle laughter greeted my comment. Oscar reached out and took the hand of the tiny, elegant woman at his side. Her face matched the profile on a rare cameo my cousin had brought back from Italy during the war. Oscar said proudly, "I'd like you to meet my wife Glenilda."

She nodded to me regally.

He continued, "When our baby was born, we had long discussions about what to name her. Glennie wanted Roxanne. I wanted Rickey. So we started calling her Rix. Just for show, we put Helen Mary on her birth certificate."

I laughed and devoured my stew.

Glenilda spoke for the first time. "Young man, sometimes you normals feel uncomfortable in our presence. Let me tell you just one thing which should put you at your ease. We little people are just as big as you are inside where it counts."

She returned to primly eating dainty bites from a serving of peach cobbler not much larger than my thumbnail.

I was introduced to three other members of the troupe who had been observing my discomfiture. Two young men were probably slightly older than me. Mick and Dan were amazing contortionists. Camille completed the company as the resident juggler.

Having finished my meal, I excused myself and headed off down the Midway to find Sharee. I passed the dwarves' show tent. The banner in front pictured a knotted Mick and Dan. They were billed as Flip and Flop. Camille juggled flaming brands. Two were suspended in the air while she held the third to her mouth. Oscar, Glenilda and Rix circled the gaudy advertisement in wedding attire.

In the distance I saw Sharee had been joined by two other figures. They were moving through languid rehearsal patterns.

She spotted me and waved. I stepped up on the platform. She introduced me to Celeste and Lola. Celeste was dressed in a soft gray gown which hung nearly to the floor. She wore a hat with a veil. Steel gray eyes peered through the slit. There was reserve in her greeting.

Lola perpetually chewed on a large wad of gum. Her ancient face belied the slim figure clad in skintight lavender slacks, a red blouse and silver snakeskin pumps with incredibly high heels. As she offered me a limp hand, she commented *sotto voce* to Sharee: "We're robbin' the cradle on this one, ain't we, honey?"

Sharee was obviously in charge. Since the other girls had arrived a day early there was no reason why we couldn't do a performance in two hours. She stepped into the show tent and emerged with a sheet of paper: "Here are your calls, Rog. Head for your digs at Hamburger Jack's. Get into your performance togs and memorize your lines."

My hand trembled as I reached for the sheet. At last I was to have a real role in a real theater production on the road!

I settled down in the front seat of Jack's truck. My eyes encountered immortal verse. Flowing across the page in beautiful script were the words:

Girls! Girls! Girls!
They shake to the east
They shake to the west
They shake right where
You want to see them shook the best.
Girls! Girls! Girls!

Uncles, bring your nephews
Fathers, bring your sons
See a little mystery and have a little fun.

From the opera halls of Europe
And the stages of old Broadway
We bring to you the world's finest
terpsichorean talent.

Step right up and see the hidden wonders of
Sharee, Celeste and Lola.
Follow them into the tent for a show

That'll make old men young
And young men older.
Girls! Girls! Girls!

I recited the lines again and again until they became a part of me.

I changed into my performance clothes. Jack had a bit of battered mirror hanging on the wall. I scarcely recognized the figure who stared bravely back. I reached down and unbuttoned my shirt to just *below* my naval.

As I headed through the closely packed lot filled with home trailers, I spotted Ramblin' Rose reclining in a lounge chair. She called out, "Yuh look great, kid. However, something ought to be done to that unruly mop of hair. I do a little barberin' on the side. Sit down here for a minute. I'll trim yuh up."

She brought out a comb, scissors, a pair of clippers and a dish towel which she pinned around my neck. I saw great clumps of hair showering to the rutted ground. In a few moments I felt positively light-headed.

I rose from the chair as she said, "You can pay me a quarter later."

Slapping me on the butt, she giggled out, "Go get 'em, kid!"

I stepped through the rear entrance of the cooch show tent. I immediately encountered Lola, who was dressed exactly like the ladies in the jungle glen. I blushed to be that close to one in the flesh. She chuckled at my discomfort.

Celeste was covered in sensuous veils. Not an inch of skin showed. As she stepped up on the stage, I was in awe at the beauty of her movement.

Sharee was garbed in a transparent, virginal, flowing white gown which revealed the fact that she had on very little underneath. I was comforted by the fact that she was wearing the familiar shoes with the clear plastic heels.

She eyed me critically and then buttoned one more button on my shirt so my naval was covered. She commented wryly, "We wouldn't want anything indecent in this show. Now, step out there and call us some customers."

I took a deep breath and stepped out on the little forestage. Behind me, sensuous music began to waft out over the crowded Midway. I set my diaphragm to strengthen the thrust of my voice and shouted, "Girls! Girls! Girls!"

Every head turned in surprise at the young, bull-like bellow clearly heard over the cacophony of carnival sounds. As I called their names, Sharee emerged from the curtains and did her brief but beautiful come-on routine. Celeste flowed over the stage like a wisp of mist. Lola slouched out, voraciously chewing her gum. She did a couple of bored bumps and grinds and slouched back through the sequined curtain which masked the entrance to the performance arena.

The sinuous music from inside the tent, the brief appearance of the performers and my constant stream of calls soon had a crowd of men gathered around the tiny platform. A gold-shirted ticket taker appeared at the entrance. As they slipped through a slit in the canvas, many of the customers glanced furtively over their shoulders to assure themselves they were avoiding the attention of girlfriends or wives.

As the afternoon wore on, I became aware of a figure haunting the edge of the gathering. The man was tall, hawk-nosed and wearing a gray flannel suit. Each time the dancers did their come-on appearance, Sharee led off. The man would stare at her with a cold, calculating look and then disappear. I wondered who he was. I would ask her about him later.

After about the hundredth repetition of my calls, I knew I had a problem. My poetic instincts were being violated by the pedestrian syllables of Lola's name, particularly when I had to pronounce them in conjunction with such glowing entities as "Sharee" and "Celeste" — both of which were classically accented on the second syllable.

We were about to begin our final performance before shutting down for dinner. A gaggle of adolescent girls gathered across the way to stare at *me.* I sensed their eyes following the line of my bare chest down the low dipping vee of my shirt — and continuing on down. They whispered among themselves.

They seemed to be engaged in hard-eyed speculation as to the probable dimensions of what was encased in the crotch of my tight pants. I suddenly felt as if I were standing on the platform naked, violated by their stares. I wondered if the dancers ever felt that way. Someday, I'd check that out.

The sun was setting. The platform was bathed in soft crimson light. The music rose behind me. The hawk-nosed man in the gray flannel suit was in his accustomed place. Distracted by a burst of sound from the motorcycle daredevils, he turned his head to look down the Midway. In the blooded light of the dying sun he looked exactly like my mindsick daddy returned from an unquiet grave. I shuddered.

The girls entered. I swung into my spiel: "Step right up and see the hidden wonders of Sharee, Celeste and Lola." When I hit the third name, I accented the final syllable and drew it out into whispered mystery: Lola-a-a-a-a-h.

She stopped her slouching progress to the front of the platform, turned on me abruptly and confronted me with a question: "What was that you just called me?"

I responded in some confusion, "L-Lola-a-a-a-a-h."

Her face was transfixed by a beatific look. She unfolded from her customary slouch to her considerable height and murmured in wonder, "That's just about the most beautiful thing anybody's ever called me."

She flowed to the front of the platform with the grace of the Firebird from Stravinsky's ballet. Silhouetted against the dying sun, she spit her huge wad of gum in a high arc over the heads of the gaping men. She stood there bathed in the sky's fading crimson, weaving to the music. She was no longer an aging cooch dancer with her sagging breasts barely encased in zebra striped fabric. She was a jungle queen.

She turned and flowed to the exit. For the first time ever, the audience applauded. I half expected that on her next entrance she would be accompanied by a sleek, chained black panther.

She had been transformed by a word as surely as I had been transformed by my new clothes. I never saw her slouch again.

The Seashore

I finished the tales at three in the morning. As I rose from my perch, I did not feel the overwhelming pain in my joints nor the tearing fatigue of the night before. I felt only joy and relief. I was creating.

I realized I hadn't been hunched over the tiny monitor. I had been sitting erect, looking into the eyes of the smiling Christ. Yes, I was writing the tales for Blind Ben and Ramblin' Rose. At the same time, I was sharing them with another Storyteller. He continued to smile.

I stretched out quietly on the bed and fell immediately asleep.

When I awakened, it was one o'clock in the afternoon. I hadn't felt this refreshed in years. I arose and went to the door. The sun was shining brightly. The beach was deserted. I splashed in the shallows.

I felt a shadow over me. I looked up. The great heron was hovering. He settled gently at water's edge. Almost faster than the eye could follow, he slashed a small whiting out of the water.

Above the clouds a fighter jet from a nearby airbase roared on a training mission. The sound jarred my memory. In the ear of my heart I heard another roar — that of a great beast.

The old heron nodded sagely, turned and walked up the beach toward the shack. He stopped and looked at me sternly and then walked a few steps further. He seemed to be informing me that I'd spent enough time at play. My daddy had told me I was never to play. The heron was giving me permission hedged with discipline.

I ran toward the hermitage passing him up. He took wing and settled on the porch just ahead of me. My mind was filled with sounds: cries of fear, a gun-bearing figure, and a tiger's roar.

Tony, the heron, had encouraged me back to work. If I focused, I might finish a third tale before five. I reached a half dozen shrimp through the window as a "thank you" gesture.

I stood under the uncertain flow of the shower and doused off the salt and sand. I headed to the computer. The brisk breeze through the open window had twisted the rosary and in the process raised up the crucifix. The torn, naked figure appeared to be nestled in the bear's embrace.

As I sat down at the keyboard, the eye on the golden shirt glowed. I felt Blind Ben See's presence urging me on.

S' TOOTH

Standing on the platform of "Ze Bra" in the intense sunlight of a late June afternoon, I watched a dust snake twist itself along the country road. A new van was arriving.

As it drew near, I saw a painting of a jungle glen similar to the one behind me. I decided such scenes must be "in" this year in terms of carnival decor.

The great vehicle crawled into the lot and nosed its way through the crowd, heading toward "Freak Show Alley." I expected to see more near-naked ladies frolicking in the foliage. Instead, a great beast crept through matted vines, palm trees and exotic flowers. The latter seemed to have been added as an afterthought by an artist-in-training. The indistinguishable splotches of color gave a tenuous, lopsided effect to the foreign locale. What at a closer view appeared to be a tiger had what was probably intended to be an orchid perched behind his left ear. Unschooled as I was in either the art of criticism or the criticism of art, I did think the awkward position of the flower called into question the intended ferociousness of the beast.

Gold curlicued letters brazenly announced: "Miss Lil and Her Genuine Saber-Toothed Tiger." I gave an amazed start. I realized I was in a prominent province of the "Land of Make-Believe." The caption's audacity stunned even me. I *knew* saber-toothed tigers had been extinct for about a million years.

The van crept into an empty slot. I saw a tiny figure descend from the maw of the great cab. He scrabbled crab-like toward the entrance to the performing area in the rear.

I had an hour free before the next show. Having been with the carnival a week, I felt like a "regular." I headed off to greet the newcomers.

I knocked on the door. A male voice called out, "Who's there?"

I responded, "My name's Rog. I'm the spieler in the cooch show. I just wanted to say 'hello.'"

The unseen figure invited me to enter: "C'mon in. Just close the door fast. I'm changin' to do a performance."

I followed his instructions. I found myself in a little cubicle with a twisted young man clad only in briefs. He stood in front of a cracked mirror about to don a fake tiger fur tunic and a dark brown fright wig. An ineptly carved caveman's club leaned against the wall.

He was less than five feet tall. Every joint in his body was grotesquely bent. Great knots rose from ill-healed bones. An image flashed into my mind. One Sunday afternoon I had slipped into a matinee at the Hollywood Motion Picture Theater in Pheasant Valley. The film of the day featured a long sequence in a medieval torture chamber. The master of villainy s-t-r-e-t-c-h-e-d victims on racks, scarred them with hot irons, shattered their limbs with a great mallet and popped out their eyeballs with his gigantic hairy thumbs. I remembered thinking at the time that my mindsick daddy had been born a few centuries too late. He would have been a natural to operate such an enterprise.

The figure before me fumbled with his costume. It slipped from his contorted fingers and fell to the van floor. I stepped forward quickly, picked up the fallen garment and held it over his head. He raised his arms.

On the wall above hung a strangely distorted crucifix. Jesus stared at us through vacant eyes set in the midst of a terror-twisted face. His fists were clenched in agony around confining spikes. As the man before me raised his arms to receive the garment, he seemed at one with the man on the cross. The garment descended, concealing the worst of his devastation.

The wall above the Christ was emblazoned with a huge multicolored circus poster. An incredibly handsome, barrel-chested young man in red, sequined tights seemed to be flying from a trapeze straight into the waiting hands of a catcher just behind the viewer. The caption read: "The Great Mario—Trapeze Artiste Extraordinaire."

Tacked on the wall next to the poster was the front page of the *Augusta Courant*. The headline screamed, "Famous Flyer Falls to Near-Death." A publicity photo of a vibrant smiling performer accompanied the article.

The silence was sliced by a sob. There was no doubt that the figure on the poster, in the newspaper and with me in the tiny room were one. Maybe he'd even modeled for the artist who carved Christ on the cross.

I turned. He offered his broken hand and choked out, "I'm Mario. Now you know everything you need to know about me."

I took his hand gently into mine and whispered, "I'm Rog. I'm all broken up inside so I guess we're a pair."

Tears came to his eyes. "I fell. The safety net tore. A guy-wire slashed my face. I hit the ground. Bones broke and muscles tore. When I came to, I prayed for death."

He glanced at the figure on the cross and commented wryly, "I'm sure he did, too.

"When I'd healed enough to leave the hospital, my Aunt Lil took me in. She was in her seventies but still touring her tiger act. I had to put her in a nursing home in Gibtown a couple of months ago. So it's just the beast and me. When he cashes in his claws and moves on to the great jungle in the sky, I don't quite know where I'll go."

Scartown had acquired a new resident.

His facial disfigurement arranged itself into a lopsided grin. Picking up his club, he turned toward a barred door. "C'mon, Rog. Give me a hand with the tiger. There's still time to work in a show before dinner."

I panicked at the invitation. My knowledge of tigers came

from that source of all wisdom: bargain matinees at the Hollywood Theater. The great beasts were mystic guardians of ruined temples in steaming jungles. They performed near-decapitation of thieving bad guys with a single swipe of razor-sharp claws. I was not about to approach a tiger.

Mario glanced over his shoulder — which was easy for him to do. His body naturally bent that way. He cajoled, "There's nothin' to be afraid of, Rog. C'mon through the door. You'll see."

I stepped hesitantly beyond the steel-barred entry door. I heard a deep rumble. I nearly leapt back where I'd come from. Mario turned on a work light. Stretched out on the van floor was an enormous, moth-eaten old tiger. He was lying on his back with his paws folded as if in prayer.

Mario knelt and began to gently scratch the tiger's exposed stomach. He said in a low voice, "C'mon, S'tooth. Another city. Another show."

He clarified, "Everybody calls him S'tooth. That's short for 'saber-toothed.'"

The great beast groaned and clumsily rolled over. It clambered slowly to its four huge paws and stretched like a gigantic house cat. Mario applauded. I followed suit, allowing myself to be drawn into the strange game.

Mario stepped to a corner cupboard and came back with something hidden in his hand. He stepped in front of S'tooth and beckoned to me. I first noticed the two gigantic teeth against the scarred palm of Mario's left hand. As I got to the head of the animal, I saw they were fastened to a small, clear plastic harness.

Mario handed me one end. Together we slipped it under his chin and over his ears. The teeth were in exactly the right place to present a bearing so ferocious that only the oldest of the old and the youngest of the young would fail to be paralyzed by fear. The ancient beast sank to the floor once more.

I laughed out loud at the sight of this splendiferous fakery. I offered an impromptu prayer of thanks to the carnival gods painted on the ticket wagon for the war effort's contribution of clear plastic to be used in sensual slippers and savage deception.

The twisted young man rolled a platform into place. The rusting wheels squealed. The old tiger cringed and put his paws over his ears. The platform contained a tank of compressed gas and a horizontal steel bar topped with a large jetted ring.

Mario pulled open the curtains on the side of the van. Through the cage bars I could see folks lining up to witness this latest addition to Freak Show Alley, eager to view a beast beyond their usual barnyard denizens.

A golden-shirted figure emerged from the crowd carrying a portable ticket podium. He was ready to collect the quarters of the curious. He quickly set up posts and stretched a semicircle of rope near the side of the van. Blind Ben See's inner eye had sensed the arrival of a new act, and he'd sent his representative to collect his share of the bounty.

Mario whispered to me, "You're a spieler. Go on out there and get me a crowd."

I queried hesitantly, "What do I say?"

He responded brusquely, "Make something up."

I slipped outside. As I stood on the stairs above the crowd, I struggled to remember any references to saber-toothed tigers from my high school biology class two years earlier.

I began my spiel:

Ladeez and gentlemen, boys and girls,
Step right up and see a world
You've never seen before:
A miraculous survivor
Of the great Ice Age
Lurking at your very door.

My melodramatic delivery of the word "lurking" sent a delicious shudder through the onlookers. The sound of my voice ringing out over the Midway drew a long line to the ticket booth. The suckers paid for the privilege of clustering inside the rope close to the great beast who had extended a long-clawed paw lazily through the bars. Those nearest the cage retreated a step or two.

I was on a roll and continued my immortal verse:

The great Mario,
Torn by the savage beast
While capturing him
In India's mystic clime
Proudly presents S'tooth,
The world's only
Gen-u-wine saber-toothed tiger
Who has survived from the dawn of time.

Mario glanced at me in amazement, grinned, gave me a thumbs-up plaudit for my performance and began the act.

He prodded S'tooth gently with his club. The old beast lumbered to its arthritic paws. Mario lighted a long-handled torch and set the gas ring aflame. He quickly stepped to the cupboard and opened the lower half, which proved to be an ice chest. He pulled out a large hunk of bloody, repulsive-looking meat.

Mario walked quickly to the far side of the performing area. He began a series of strange whistling calls. S'tooth crouched. With amazing grace he leaped through the ring of fire and landed at Mario's feet.

He violently tore the proffered food from his keeper's hand, turned and stalked his way toward the audience. Frightened onlookers shrank back, inwardly speculating about the strength of the intervening bars. In the imaginations of their hearts they could see a bit of their own anatomy dangling from the gleaming white teeth.

S'tooth carefully laid his reward on the floor and stared menacingly at the huddled mass of fear before him. He gathered his flagging strength and gave a horrendous, roof-raising territorial roar.

A communal scream echoed from the tightly clustered crowd. They turned and scattered down the Midway, having gotten the scare of a lifetime, a quarter's worth of fear.

Mario pulled the curtain. The show was over.

I returned to the platform of "Ze Bra." The summer heat and horrendous humidity did not seem to dampen the enthusiasm of the crowds for the carnival's provision of multilevel unreality. Thunderheads began boiling up far out on the plains. I hoped for a brief shower to cool the sweltering air. I pitied the dancers in the oven-like tent which extended out from the main van to form the performance area. However, the shouts, whistles and catcalls from the crowd of leering men were as raucous as ever.

Evening came. The heat remained, accentuating the smells of Hamburger Jack's pungent offerings intertwined with the incense of caramel corn and the rank odor of the overheated old tiger. I longed for the arrival of midnight when relief would come in the shape of a cooling ride.

Guido the Gimp operated the Star of Bethlehem Ferris wheel. When the carnival closed down for the night, he'd let all comers mount the great wheel's passenger carriers. He'd set it at top speed and twirl us until the sweat of the day evaporated in cooling waves that made us shiver.

After the final show the dancers slipped off exhausted to their beds. I closed up the performing area and headed for the ride. My usual companions were already involved in card games or, bleary-eyed with fatigue, stumbled toward their trailers.

I paused to greet Mario and S'tooth and ask the crooked man to accompany me. Mario invited me in. The old tiger was pacing nervously in his cage. He exhibited unaccustomed vigor.

Mario decided to remain with his ancient charge to see if he could quiet him. S'tooth paused at the flimsily barred door to the living quarters and leaned against it. Mario extended his twisted hand through the protective grating to scratch the twitching ears and the swayed back of his jungle terror. A low purring growl of pleasure came from the throat of the becalmed beast, matching the roll of the approaching thunder.

As I departed, Mario asked me to leave the door open with the hope of getting a bit of breeze through the van which might relieve both man and tiger.

I rushed to the wheel, not wanting Guido to begin without me. He was standing alone by the controls. He managed some garbled sounds through his unrepaired harelip and cleft palate which I interpreted to mean that I was his only late-night "customer."

I climbed aboard. The motor ground wearily to a start, sounding as if it too had experienced a hard day in the heat and needed a night of rest. I felt myself lifted toward the stars. From the height of the great wheel the island of light below looked like a distant planet. I was plunged down into Scartown, and then lifted once again toward the full moon which fought the approaching clouds. The storm was closer than I thought.

Suddenly the night sky was shattered by multiple bolts of lightning. The resultant crash of thunder threatened to explode my eardrums.

Three things happened simultaneously with the Olympian clap — the power failed, plunging the carnival into darkness. S'tooth gave a panicked roar which shook the surrounding countryside, rivaling any sound created for a Saturday matinee horror film. The motor below sputtered to a halt as I found myself marooned at the apex of the Ferris wheel.

There was pandemonium below. I heard wood crashing to the ground and Hamburger Jack's high-pitched scream, "The tiger's loose! The tiger's loose!"

The cry was taken up across the lot. I sensed I was floating above swirling, irrational frenzy. I knew what'd happened. Fearing the thunderclap, S'tooth had thrown himself against the grating. It had given way. He slithered quickly out the door I'd left open.

Hamburger Jack's stand was next door. S'tooth knocked aside the serving counter and helped himself to a bit of calming meat before rushing through the lot trying to escape the repetitive claps and bolts from the angry heavens.

The screams below mounted. I heard the surly voice of Snaggle-Tooth Tommy, my least favorite roustabout, proclaim, "Calm down, everbody. I'm a'gittin' my rifle!"

I tried to call out that the great cat was harmless. The roar from the sky and the screams from below drowned out my voice of reason.

The storm passed as quickly as it came. Not a drop of rain fell. The current returned. The troubled world below burst into light.

The scene will ever be etched in my mind like a museum painting: frenzied figures frozen in their places expecting to be torn by sharp claws extending from primal paws.

The only movement came from Snaggle-Tooth Tommy who rushed helter-skelter with his rifle held at ready, randomly threatening the guilty and innocent. His single great yellow tooth dangled from his receding upper jaw and was bathed constantly in tobacco juice as it glowed viciously in the harsh illumination of the work lights.

Silence gradually descended as everyone's attention was captured by the tableau on the Fun House platform bathed in greens and blues from the Star of Bethlehem Ferris wheel. Blind Ben See reclined calmly on his peeling golden throne. The great tiger was trembling in his lap, his rear paws resting on the worn floor, his front paws around the old carney's neck. Ben was scratching S'tooth gently behind his left ear.

The magic of the scene enacted before the Mirror of Truth drew the carnival folk together. There was a long silence broken only by a momentary command from Ben: "Tommy, put down that silly gun. You might hurt somebody."

Tommy sheepishly lowered his weapon.

As I viewed the panorama from the top of the wheel, I couldn't help feeling I was in church.

The sermon was a two-liner from the old carney: "Folks, I want you to remember one important thing from tonight. Most times the beings we fear the most are most afraid of us."

Mario slipped to the platform. S'tooth unwound himself from Ben's embrace, rushed across the platform and put his front paws on his keeper's shoulders, knocking him to the floor. The two friends wrestled. Their game was magnified in the great mirrors.

The onlookers burst into laughter. As the sounds of their merriment drifted up to my still point in the turning world, the universe seemed momentarily balanced by sounds of joyous relief.

The great wheel rotated me once again to the moonlit earth.

The Seashore

It was 4:30 in the afternoon. I put the computer on "print" and watched the pages clatter forth in neat folds. Picking up the sheets, I realized that one of the stories I'd written was about Mario and another introduced Celeste. I could feel the next story forming in my soul's eye. Celebrating my creative output, I pulled on my Speedo, cutoffs and golden shirt. I heard the blare of the Chrysler's novelty horn playing "Good Night Ladies." I was sorry Blind Ben and Ramblin' Rose were picking me up. I needed a good half-hour walk down the beach. I made a mental note to tell them I'd join them there tomorrow.

As I climbed into the back seat, I noticed two things: a sly smile dancing at the corners of Blind Ben's mouth and a Coleman lantern on the seat beside me.

I queried, "What's with the lantern?"

Ben responded, "Since you've been so prolific the past twenty-four hours, I didn't want to miss any of your profundity with the arrival of darkness."

I protested, "But how did you know . . . ?"

Then I remembered the shirt and the carnival lot myth of the eye. Ramblin' Rose's laughter pealed out.

We arrived at our theater in the sand. I was excited about performing. Rog, the psychological side show freak, was beginning to face his family ghosts with more aplomb.

I helped Ben from the car. He seemed to have less physical energy, but his voice glowed as he shared, "I've been looking forward to this all day. God, kid, I'm glad you found us. As we fade away, it's nice to know we meant something good to somebody."

I settled him on his golden throne and held him for a long moment.

A warm, gentle breeze blew off the sea. Rose and I carved out places on the sun-heated sand. I read "Paradise Gained," "Two Transformations" and "S'tooth." My listeners kept erupting into gales of laughter.

Ben said, "Boy, you got some memory. If what you're writing isn't true, it ought to be. I wish you could keep in your head that word 'transformation.' A new set of clothes for you and a new name for Lola meant a new lease on life for both of you. But these stories you've written now are no less agents of transformation. If you let them, they can take you a giant step along your journey to resolve the stuff with your daddy. If other folks haunted by pain ever get the chance to read them, they might be helped along on their journeys."

He paused for a moment and listened to the sound of the sea. Rose said in a voice tinged with wonder, "Look over there! That beautiful big heron's come to pay us a visit!"

Ben turned his sightless eyes in the direction he sensed from her voice. Tony, the heron, had settled down at the edge of the surf a few yards away.

Ben whispered, "I feel inside like we've been joined by an old friend."

I said quietly, "We have."

No further explanation was needed.

Blind Ben continued, "You make me out a lot better than I ever thought I was. I live with three haunting sisters: Adultery, Betrayal and Guilt. You know the story of how I lost my sight. I've spent my whole life trying to help a few folks like you try to forgive themselves and everybody who's hurt them. Having listened to your tales, I'll die a lot easier in my mind."

Rose reached up, patted his hand and laid her head on his knee: "I don't want you talkin' 'bout dyin' as if you was goin' off and doin' it by yerself. Remember, we promised each other we'd hang out tuhgether."

He changed the subject: "Since you're down there, pull off my shoes and socks, Rose. I want to feel the water flowing over my feet."

She did as he requested and at the same time rolled the pant legs of his shiny dark suit up to his knees. He rose from his great chair, staggered for a moment and then regained his balance as I grabbed his elbow. He shrugged off my hand and shuffled slowly to the water's edge.

I stayed at his side. The wavelets whispered in above his ankles. As each surge touched him, his knees bent slightly, and he swayed to the rhythm of the sea in the same pattern as the watching heron.

He said softly, "I'd like to just stand here doing my little prayer dance and let the water slowly draw me into the Mystery. When I was a preacher man, I didn't know diddly-squat about the Sacred at the heart of everything. In the carnival, it kept surprising me. Here, it sneaks up on me, and I have time to pursue that strangeness — or that Stranger."

Night tumbled down quickly. I led Ben back. Rose had lighted the Coleman lantern. I eased him to the sand.

I said, "I think it's time for a love story."

Rose brightened: "That'd be real nice."

She snuggled Ben in her lap.

Mario and Celeste

As the caravan of wildly decorated trucks pulled into another tiny town, the usual line of tight-lipped, disapproving adults and rejoicing children greeted the carnival's arrival. We passed the village road marker: *Munroville, population 1,002.*

The performance lot was dry and level. We set up the show in record time. Mario and Sharee had arranged with Blind Ben to park our vans side by side since both featured similar jungle scenes in their decor. It also meant that if we timed it right I could spiel both shows.

Older carneys kept assuring me that I had the potential of being one of the best spielers in the business. If I really minded my "p's" and "q's," I might one day become a circus ringmaster. My dreams took a new turn.

Having finished setting up "Ze Bra," I crossed the organized chaos of the emerging carnival to give Mario a hand.

He greeted me: "We've both finished early. Let's stretch our legs and see the sights in this major metropolis."

We strolled down main street. Our golden-orange shirts drew suspicious stares from the inhabitants of the drab little town.

Three small girls were skipping rope in front of the Five-and-Dime store. Seeing Mario, one of them shrilled, "Here comes the boogie man. Run! Run! Run!"

They scampered away, giggling nervously in mock terror. Mario cringed at my side.

We passed the village barbershop. Gold curlicued letters on the window proclaimed: "Come Clean with Barber Bert." A small, primitively scrawled sign beneath the other proclaimed the availability of showers for ten cents. Mario said, "Let's stop and take advantage of the possibility of getting really clean for once. I'm tired of sponging myself off in a pan of water heated on my hot plate. I'll even treat you, kid. It'll be partial payment for all the times you've helped me."

We walked two blocks back to the lot, and both of us picked up a change of clothes.

We stepped into the shop and made our wishes known. Mario extended two dimes to the barber, who eyed us suspiciously through tiny glasses perched on the end of his sharp nose. He reached for a couple of worn towels with raveling edges and shoved them reluctantly into our hands with a warning word: "I'll be back in a minute and check up on you two. I don't allow no funny business between guys."

The barber returned to his task of completing a crew cut on a gravelly-voiced customer who loudly proclaimed, "I always hate to see them damned carneys hit town. They're nothing but a bunch of thieves and sex freaks. I hope you ain't got nothin' stealable in yer back room."

We stepped quickly away from the offending dialogue and into a dark hallway. A dangling sign indicated that showers were through a door on the left.

We were greeted by a grim concrete room smelling of mildew. It contained two worn benches, a rickety little wicker table and two rusting, once-white metal shower cabinets with no curtains. They shared a small bar of Lava soap.

We stripped quickly, turned on the faucets and stepped into high pressure flows of glorious hot water, which partially redeemed the sordid surroundings.

We stayed in the showers until we were waterlogged. Staggering out, we quickly discovered the towels left much to be desired in terms of absorbing moisture.

We spread them on the benches to avoid puncturing our

posteriors with splinters and sat waiting for the steam to clear. I rose and opened a high window so that circulating air might dry us off.

Mario stared at me with tears in his eyes. He choked out, "I'm sorry, Rog. Looking at you made me remember that before the fall I once had a body as straight and rounded as yours. Now audiences snicker when I walk into the tiger cage, women look the other way, men stare in derision, suspecting my privates were destroyed in the accident, and children run from the boogie man.

"I'd always dreamed of loving a woman and being loved, of having a child and swinging it to sleep on a low-mount trapeze bar.

"Now, that's a stupid dream. Nobody could ever love me as I am. You know what I wish, Rog? I wish old S'tooth would go mad some night, clamp his teeth around my neck and puncture my jugular vein. I'd bleed to death before the gaping crowd. They'd really get their quarter's worth!"

Before I could reply, the customer from the barber chair burst into the room. He exploded loudly, "Barber Bert sent me back to send you on your way. He says yuh've outstayed yer welcome. It's a damn good thing I come when I did. Two nekkid men sittin' for half an hour starin' at one another's privates. Hard to tell what else has gone on between yuh.

"I can understand such activity from little old crookedy Gus there. Yer prob'ly pertty hard up fer action. No woman in her right mind would come near yuh.

"But the kid there's another matter. Hey, boy. Send yer friend back to the lot. We'll just take a little shower together and get each other real clean, and we'll see what might jist happen."

His right hand had strayed to his groin. In my mind's eye I was stretched on the corncrib concrete with my rampaging father poised above me.

Simultaneously, Mario and I leapt toward the rickety table and grabbed our stacks of clean clothes. I got into mine with record speed. Mario moved more slowly. I helped him with his shirt and buckled his belt.

My shoulder was impaled by the customer's steely fingers. I glanced up. Barber Bert had not gotten around to shaving him.

A week's stubble mottled his sunken cheeks. His eyes were canaled with red. I smelled stale whiskey on his breath.

He whispered, "Don't be scared, kid. I'd be real gentle."

The door to the shower room burst open once more. Two huge, gold-shirted figures entered, the eyes on their pockets glowing. Hamburger Jack had a knife in his hand. He said softly, "Blind Ben said he 'sensed' the two of you might be in trouble in the barber shop shower room. His inner sight was right as usual."

Al the Alligator Man's scaled face was menacing in the dim light as he towered over the customer. He grabbed him quickly by the neck and shoved him backward into a shower. He turned on the cold water and held the floundering figure's face near the cascading head as he ground out through his clenched teeth, "Us 'gators like water. Hope this will cool some sense into that drunken head of yours and into any other part of your anatomy that happens to be out of line."

As Al released his hold, the terrorized figure sank limply to the shower floor, the cascading water continuing to choke him. He began to cough.

Jack had quickly bundled our soiled clothes. We headed out through the shop. Barber Bert was frozen against a flyspecked display of hair tonic, a towel around his neck, an open razor in his left hand.

He rasped out, "I'll slit the throat of anybody what comes near me."

Alligator Al moved slowly toward him. The razor was still poised in space. Al ground out, "I've already soiled my hands once today. I wouldn't want to do it again."

He grabbed the dangling end of Bert's towel and whipped it off with a velocity that left a fabric burn on the neck of the petrified man. Al dried the shower water from his face and hands. He threw the towel back at the shuddering figure. It caught on the tip of the razor and dangled there.

Bert looked like the statue of a crazed barber as he stood immobile as the life-sized wooden Indian which graced the opposite corner of the shop.

We walked back to the lot. Jack put a protective arm around my shoulders. Al matched his lengthy steps to Mario's crippled hop.

We passed the Fun House platform. The sun reflected off the Mirror of Truth, giving Ben's seated figure a glaring aureole like that of an avenging angel. I said quietly, "Thanks, Ben."

He responded, "I always protect my own."

Mario and I grinned at each other. It felt real good to be somebody's own. As I write this memoir, I wonder if I should capitalize the "S" on "Somebody's."

Later in the afternoon as Sharee, Celeste and Lola were doing their "come on and come in," I saw the hawk-nosed man in the gray flannel suit leaning against a light pole, staring at Sharee in that peculiar way.

My attention was diverted by a sharp movement on the platform of the tiger act. Mario had been waiting for me to finish at "Ze Bra" so I could step next door and gather a crowd for the sleepy S'tooth. He swung his emaciated body abruptly around and headed in to don his caveman costume. He was weeping.

A few moments later I stepped unannounced into his little living room at the end of the van outside the great cage. The fake fur guise was crumpled on the floor. He was leaning against the wall beneath the poster of the perfect flyer poised forever between earth and sky. Sobs tore his battered rib cage.

I put a hand gently on his shoulder. He flung it off like a petulant child. I knelt and forcibly molded his twisted form against my body as Gletha, John and Tony had done so many times in the midst of my battering.

I queried, "What brought all this on — beyond your usual sense of being worthless?"

He muttered through his abating sobs, "It was watching her."

"Who?"

He responded softly, "Celeste."

Not even the Virgin Mary's name could have been pronounced more reverently. He continued, "She never reveals even a touch of flesh. Her face is shadowed behind her veil. I've known a lot of beautiful women. They used to cluster around me in my flyer days. I could have whoever I wanted. Now all I can do is fantasize the perfection beneath the flow of fabric. She moves with such exquisite grace.

"I wish that I might one day hold her in my arms. Imagination is fine, but I long for love encased in flesh."

He shook himself brusquely from my hug, continuing, "Enough of this nonsense. We've got a show to do."

He stepped to the washstand in the corner, poured water into the chipped enameled pan and doused his head. I dropped his costume over his shoulders and deliberately slapped the fright wig on backwards, the stringy hair dangling over his face. He glanced in the cracked mirror. The quiet of the tiny room was exploded by his laughter.

As the chuckles subsided, he seemed to unfold a bit. I had a momentary glimpse of the perfect athlete postered above.

We stepped through the grilled door, awakened S'tooth and performed our usual fear-filled extravaganza.

That night, at Mario's invitation, I moved my bedding from the cramped quarters of Hamburger Jack's truck to his more spacious living room. Mario was glad to be relieved of some of the duties involved in caring for the ancient beast. I carried water with more ease than he.

Mario casually affirmed that it wasn't bad having company. He paused for a moment and then warmed my heart by commenting, "You're the first person I've let near me since the fall."

A few days later I was performing another of my community tasks — passing out mail. I paused at Celeste's trailer. For the second time I was delivering a letter to her from something called "The Hartford Insurance Company." I was fascinated by the sources of the carneys' mail. Most states and a dozen foreign countries were represented within our fragile band of make-believe.

I knocked. There was no answer. Supposing her to be out on the lot, I opened the door and stepped in as I'd done before, intending to put the letter on her little table.

I saw her. The curtains on her sleeping space were open.

She was standing sideways staring over her left shoulder at her reflection in a full-length mirror. The midmorning sun poured through a window, spotlighting every curve of her body. She was naked.

In that instant of illumination I saw every inch of her skin was cracked and furrowed like the bottom of a drought-haunted pond parched dry by the fiery winds of summer. Her mouth was twisted to one side which explained the lisp behind her veils on those rare occasions when she spoke. Her right nipple drooped at the end of a particularly angry scar.

She spotted my distant reflection. She gasped and grabbed an oriental robe hanging on a chair back. She quickly donned it, turned and floated toward me with that consummate grace which transformed the cooch show stage a dozen times a day. She held her left arm in front of her face. The wings of the elegant crane embroidered on her robe embraced her protectively as she advanced.

She lisped softly, "You've seen me now, Rog. Why are you still standing there? The last man who saw me nude ran retching from my presence."

She was quite near me. I was mesmerized by her eyes. Though the lids were crooked, the brown depths of frightened iridescence reminded me of the magnificent eyes of a fawn Gletha and I had rescued from a swamp years before.

My stammer returned for a moment: "Celeste, j-j-just because you've been hurt doesn't m-m-mean that I've g-g-got to run away. Wh-wh-what in the world happened?"

Tears flowed through rivulets veining her scarred cheeks. She sobbed out, "I was dancing in a little Tennessee town. There'd been a lot of objection to the performance's 'immorality' by some who called themselves 'Christians.' In their eyes we dancers were responsible for destroying families.

"One of the protesters set fire to the stage end of the tent, sensing himself to be the chosen instrument of God's holy wrath.

"The men who were watching the show rushed to the only exit. In the process they flung us backwards toward the flames.

Two dancers died. There have been many days when I wished the gift of death had been mine.

"The arsonist was jailed. Crowds of his supporters swirled all night by torchlight, surrounding his place of incarceration and demanding that he be freed. In the morning a judge up for reelection released him.

"I was told later that his friends led the erstwhile prisoner in triumph to a nearby church. They shouted prayers of praise to God for giving him courage to rid the world of a corner of Satan's filth.

"My cousin is a lawyer. He managed to get me a small settlement. Twice a month I receive twenty dollars from the Hartford Insurance Company. I can't live on that. When I'd healed as much as I'm ever going to heal, I knew I had to dance again.

"Lola's sister was fatally burned in the fire. She died in the hospital bed next to mine. Lola'd come and see me whenever she was in the area. The day I could move again we teamed up with Sharee to perform 'Ze Bra.' I became the Mystery Lady of the cooch show circuit.

"You know, I think our show has real class. It's the animals who come to rape us with their eyes who are classless.

"Well, Rog, now you have a choice piece of carnival gossip to share with the company."

I responded quickly, "Oh, don't worry, Celeste. I'm the world's champion secret keeper!"

Her fawn's eyes clouded again. "Now that you've seen me, maybe you can understand how lonely it is inside these scars, particularly when it's obvious that nobody would ever want to touch me in love as a woman hungers to be touched."

I mumbled something about how someone could fall in love with her beautiful eyes if she'd only let down her face veil so we could see them. She countered: "Maybe I'll do that on Halloween when it's permissible to scare people!"

We shared a bit of nervous laughter. I continued on my route.

A few days later I noticed Mario standing on the platform by S'tooth's cage, watching the terpsichorean trio inviting their audience into fantasyland. Was it my imagination, or did Celeste insert an extra sequence of veiled sensuality as she performed her "turn"?

On the opposite side of the burgeoning crowd, the hawk-nosed man in the gray flannel suit pried his gaze off Sharee for a moment as Celeste left the stage doing a series of incredible cancan steps.

The two men framed that scene forever in my mind: the lot shadowed by the Star of Bethlehem Ferris wheel, the ear bombarded by the tinseled tones of Grandma Nell at the carousel, the conflicting cacophony of spielers' calls and the two of them rooted on either side — twin pillars of love and lust.

It began in the cook tent that very night. Mario dined with the dwarf troupe from the first day he arrived on the lot. His convoluted body made him appear not much larger than they. He often kidded Oskar that he was going to train Mick and Dan to do a miniature trapeze act while Camille juggled below them on a high wire.

On this particular evening the dwarves had eaten early. Someone missed a cue in the afternoon performance. Oskar's particular traits of perfectionist and benevolent tyrant were aroused. An extra rehearsal was called before the evening performance.

Mario settled next to Celeste and began to eat in his peculiar fashion necessitated by having to hold his silverware between his little finger and its neighbor. At one point his fork slipped and a glob of spaghetti sauce ended up on his nose. For an instant he looked the classic clown. Giggles erupted from beneath the veil on his right. His blushing response almost matched the color of the sauce.

Like a mother caring for a child, Celeste tenderly removed the offending stain from his face with a quick motion of her napkin. Discomfited by her involuntary act, she rose quickly and fled through the gathering dusk toward her trailer.

Mario and I were left alone at the rough plank table. I poured us each another cup of incredibly strong coffee Ramblin' Rose guaranteed would keep every carney alert until 1 A.M.

He sat frozen in reverie, his cup halfway to his lips. I commented wryly, "Either drink it or put it down. Otherwise you'll slop it across your face and add burns to your other beauty marks."

He looked at me in dumb amazement and crooned, "She laughed at me and then she touched me. She seemed unafraid to touch me. It's the first time I've been touched by a woman since the fall."

He was silent for a long moment and then continued, "I've been watching her ever since I hit the show."

I inserted, "So I've noticed."

He retorted, "I hoped I hadn't been that obvious. I can't stop wondering what's beneath the veils. I've fantasized every beautiful face I've ever seen. I've had a lot of women over the years, but none of them ever moved with the grace of Celeste. There's something incredibly beautiful there."

I responded, "Further beneath the veils than you'd ever imagine."

He looked at me strangely, but didn't press me. Sliding stiffly off the bench, he hobbled into the night.

After the final show, Celeste stopped me as I was headed to help Hamburger Jack clean up. She put an arm trustingly through mine and whispered, "I made a fool of myself in the cook tent tonight. I should never have touched Mario or laughed at him. He's been watching me for days. I used to be something of a tease before the fire. Some of my old self snuck out. I've felt I had to hold it all in since this happened."

I felt a ghost of celebration rising in me. If I played it right, maybe I could help each of them discover who was hidden amidst the physical devastation.

A second hope pursued the first. Maybe someday somebody'd help me discover I really wasn't "no damn good" like my daddy always told me.

I responded carefully, "There wouldn't be nothing wrong if you placed yourself in the way of some casual conversation. You never know what you might find out."

The sun was just appearing over the horizon the next

morning as Mario and I followed the enticing aroma of frying bacon toward the cook tent. In the distance I saw the curtains on Celeste's window move slightly. As we came abreast of her trailer, she stepped out. I greeted her warmly. Mario couldn't get his mouth open.

A bird on a branch above us broke into an incredible round of trills. Celeste stopped and said, "How beautiful! I wonder what kind of bird it is?"

Mario said instantly, "It's a pileated Parker's warbler."

Celeste responded wonderingly, "How do *you* know so much about birds?"

"I learned from my father. He'd always wanted to be an ornithologist. My grandfather insisted that our family had been aerialists for a hundred and fifty years, and he was not to break the tradition. My dad was killed in Canton, Ohio, when a tornado toppled our big top.

"I was twelve. At his graveside, my grandfather put his arm around me and said that I was to become the world's greatest flyer and carry on 'the tradition.' Well, I sure have carried on the disaster part."

Tears dappled his cheeks.

Celeste said quickly, "Tell me more about that beautiful sound."

I slipped away, leaving them to discuss bird song in the first rays of the rising sun.

It was Oskar, who, one morning at breakfast, commented on the increasing time the two of them spent together: "I was getting used to an additional member of our company. It was the first time a great one reshaped by fate had ever joined us. I'm glad that real coming together happens inside folks. On the outside it looks like the mating of a tower and a toadstool!"

His comment whirled in my mind all day as I stood on the platform and gathered the show crowds. They were "mating"? I'd grown up watching bulls cover cows, stallions their mares and rams their ewes. I'd heard my mother's screams in the night as my daddy did whatever he did to her in the darkness. I knew what my daddy'd done to me had nothing to do with mating.

I watched the customers grinning at the dancers, their lips parted, their breath coming a little faster. They entered the tent with butt-slapping, groin-grabbing camaraderie. The scene was always shadowed by the hard-eyed stare of the hawk-nosed man in the gray flannel suit.

I looked over at the tiger show. Mario crouched there waiting for the entrance of Celeste. His face broke into that beatific grin which marked his daily transfiguration. She moved to the front of the platform, stood stock still for a moment, and then slowly raised her left hand toward heaven. She'd attached tiny bells to her fingers. She moved only her wrist. Her fingers fluttered like the wings of a captive bird. A pure crystal sound filled a rare moment of silence while Grandma Nell took a break from the calliope. I thought it was the most sensual act I'd seen on the cooch show platform.

The rare mood was shattered by a raucous shout from the back of the crowd: "Cut the artsy-crafty stuff, girlie, and twirl those boobs, or we ain't comin' into yer show."

Lola entered quickly and gave the crowd what they wanted while Celeste shuddered off the stage. I glanced toward Mario. His fists were clenched angrily. He glared at the offender, who was being loudly congratulated by back-slapping buddies as they headed for the performance entrance.

All that day the Midwestern sun blazed unrelentingly down. Performers and crew were miserable. We had to keep sprinkling asthmatic old S'tooth with cool water. The electrical supply of the little town was strained by the number of fans which appeared in show tents.

That night someone discovered a nearby stream sporting a swimming hole. Word spread quickly that a community dip was in the offing at one in the morning.

I didn't plan to go. My fear of water was still strong. Daddy threw me from a worn wooden boat one time too many in his attempts to force me to swim. Mario insisted he wouldn't expose his battered body to the casual stares of the bathers.

The moon shown with particular intensity, enhaloed with dust from the sun-shattered earth. We sat outside the van in the cooling night air and played gin rummy for awhile and then went to bed.

I was awakened by the quiet laughter of returning swimmers. I heard Blind Ben's voice in their midst. They'd been properly chaperoned.

When it was quiet again, Mario slipped from his cot. I raised up on an elbow and queried, "Are you okay?"

"I can't sleep," he replied. "I'm going to take a walk. Don't worry about me."

I heard him return. From the position of the moon shining through the window, I judged he'd been gone a couple hours. He paused in the golden light and looked down the alley formed by the carnival transportation vehicles. He stripped off his clothes. I could see his shirt was damp and his hair was soaked.

I queried, "You went for a swim alone after everybody'd left?"

He responded quietly, "I wasn't alone. Celeste was with me."

Something inside me clutched in fearful anticipation as I whispered, "So, you know?"

"Yes. We saw each other's stories. There were two granite outcroppings in the middle of the great pool. We each swam out to one and climbed up to its flat top.

"I turned and let her see every battered bone, torn muscle and deformed limb in my body. She turned and let me see her fire-scarred flesh. We both knew the other would swim in stark terror to the opposite side of the pool. Instead, we slipped into the water, swam into each other's arms and embraced for a long, long time."

I blurted out, "Did you mate?"

His laughter exploded. He leaped across the room and pummeled me flat in my bedroll.

His face was half serious, half amused as he said, "Mating was not on our minds. We simply needed to feel the healing touch of somebody else who cared. I'll be honest. It's the first time in my life I've been naked with a woman and haven't 'mated.' It's also the first time in my life I've really been in love. Everything's in a rather different perspective.

"Well, let's get some sleep. I feel like a brand new man inside."

I envied him. I wondered if I'd ever feel like that.

From his cot I heard his warm chuckle and a final word, "By the way, Rog. You can stop worrying about me. My testicles weren't crushed nor my penis broken in the fall. When the right time comes, I'll be able to mate just fine."

I was glad my bedroll lay outside the trail of light cast by the exquisite lovers' moon. I didn't want Mario to see my blush.

The show folk were quick to see that offstage, Mario and Celeste walked the lot together. At first she towered over him. Then it was noticed that Mario was walking taller. His head which had always been bowed to the ground lifted a bit each day. The roustabouts kidded him good-naturedly about forcing his head up so he could "keep an eye on the mystery lady."

One evening when I'd finished my duties at "Ze Bra," I paused to sate my late-night appetite with a burger from Jack's stall. I was a working man. I could even afford to pay for it.

Jack leaned on the counter and commented wryly, "Unless I miss my guess, that roommate of yours is in love. Tell him to come and see me if he ever even thinks about getting married. I'll prepare him for the pain that always hangs in there under the joy — and the joy that keeps itself wound around the pain."

As I walked back toward the tiger van, I passed Sharee's trailer. I heard her burst out laughing. I called out, "Hey, Sharee, what's so funny?"

The words were no sooner out of my mouth when I clutched. What if she were entertaining a guest? In a traveling world where privacy is at a premium, one tried to respect a neighbor's space — at least that was what Blind Ben grilled into us when we had "company meetings."

She responded, "Rog, step in here. You've got to hear this."

I hesitated. She'd never invited me into her private quarters. Lots of people were passing back and forth. I wouldn't want any of them to get the "wrong idea."

Curiosity overcame me. I stepped inside.

I gasped. The walls of the trailer were lined with books! I felt like I'd stepped into a library on wheels. She was sitting in a rocking chair with a volume in her hands. She saw my surprise and offered an explanation: "I hope you can keep a secret. I don't let many people into this piece of my world. I don't want anybody in the carnival family to think that I feel myself superior to them.

"You see, I have no intention of spending my life as a cooch show queen. In the fall, I'll return to the University of Minnesota and finish my doctorate in English Literature."

I wasn't sure what a "doctorate" was, but for once in my life I kept my mouth shut and let her continue.

"I really want to be a writer. My family always spoke in hushed, distasteful tones about my dad's sister, Aunt Emilia. She 'worked' in a carnival. Nobody would ever say what she did. During her rare visits as I was growing up, I became fascinated by her. She had the most beautiful long blonde hair I'd ever seen.

"When I was little, she'd pick me up and dance with me. I've loved to dance ever since. When anyone dropped by, my parents would introduce her as a 'physical education instructor.' She would smile wryly and never correct them.

"One day just before classes were over last spring, Emilia arrived at our house in Minneapolis. She was driving 'Ze Bra' and pulling this little house trailer behind it. I was home alone.

"She was very, very ill. Her body was riddled with cancer. She danced with veils to cover her missing breasts. She'd wintered with other carneys in Gibsonton, Florida, and had gotten all the treatment possible in the Ringling Hospital nearby.

"She sensed that death was not far away. She'd contracted with Lola and Celeste for this season. She didn't want to die alone. She mustered enough strength to drive clear across the country.

"I put her to bed. When my folks arrived, they were shocked to find the garish van parked in their respectable neighborhood. However, they're good people. When they saw Emilia's condition, they forgave everything from the past and immediately became caregivers.

"I got permission to park the van in a warehouse lot. As I drove to my destination, a plan evolved. Maybe I could do research on carnival life by living it. I'd have real material for a novel.

"I sat by her bedside every moment I could, letting her ramble on about her thirty-five years in show business. I took notes.

"She'd describe the girlie show routines. I'd dance them out in her bedroom. She'd correct me.

"Three weeks later she died in my arms. Her final words to me were, 'Keep dancin'.'"

Tears were streaming down Sharee's cheeks. She whispered, "I'll dedicate my novel to her."

To distract her from her sorrow, I inquired, "Will I be in your novel?"

She laughed as she dried her tears and said, "Sure, Rog. I might even make you the hero."

That embarrassed me, so I asked, "What were you laughing about when I walked by earlier?"

She responded, "Remember that package you delivered to me during mail time this morning? It was this new book of poems: *The Collected Poetry of W. H. Auden.* I was reading a selection called "Songs and Other Musical Pieces." Listen to the first four lines:

O stand, stand at the window
As the tears scald and start;
You must love your crooked neighbor
With your crooked heart.

She laughed in sheer delight. I joined her.

I said goodnight and headed for the tiger van. The poetry rolled over and over in my mind. I thought of someone else who needed to hear it. It seemed these lines needed to be painted on the canvas entrance to Scartown.

As I entered my shared quarters, I heard S'tooth's *basso profundo* purr echoing from his cage. I looked through the barred entrance. Mario was crouched on the floor, cradling the head of the old beast in his lap and scratching the striped ears. There was a faraway look in his eyes. Love's silly grin played around his lips.

I stepped into the cage and knelt down to scratch the ancient beast behind his other ear. Mario looked at me dreamily and said, "I want to ask Celeste to marry me, but I just don't have the courage to offer her my batteredness."

I said sagely, "Well, I might be able to help you with your decision."

A bemused, "How?" broke from his lips.

I continued: "Sharee just shared four lines of poetry that might assist you in making up your mind."

He looked doubtful: "I've never been much into poetry, but go ahead. I'm open to anything."

Trying to remember every dramatic inflection I'd been taught in high school theater, I declaimed:

O stand, stand at the window
As the tears scald and start;
You must love your crooked neighbor
With your crooked heart.

Mario looked at me strangely. Without a word he scrambled to his feet and left the van. S'tooth lifted his head and growled menacingly at the retreating figure as if he were objecting to the possibility of another living being entering Mario's life.

Two hours later I was awakened by a long peal of laughter. The angle of the moon pouring through the window indicated it was about 3 A.M. The golden light illumined the great poster and the hunched figure standing beneath it. I struggled sleepily to my feet.

"Mario," I mumbled, "did Celeste tell you a joke?"

He turned, opened his arms and embraced me in a great bear hug. I dropped my gangling form to my knees so we could be on the same level.

"I recited the poem to her. She told me that she loved me very much — enough to risk marrying me."

For a moment he stared over my shoulder at the poster. He whispered, "I'll never climb to the peak of the Big Top again, but tonight my heart's on the flying trapeze."

He released me. Taking me by the arm, he continued, "Come

over to the window where the light is brighter. I have something to show you."

Reaching into his pocket, he said with a touch of wonder in his voice, "I was walking home and I met Ramblin' Rose. She said she can never sleep through a full moon. I shared my news with her. She cried and then said she had something for me. She went inside her trailer. When she came back she handed me these, saying she'd taken them off the day her husband slashed her. She'd been waiting for years to find somebody to give them to who might really find love with another."

He opened his hand. Nestled in his palm were two incredible diamonds flaming in the moonlight. They were mounted on strangely crafted rings. Three slender strands of gold had been woven together in two perfect circles.

The wedding was set for 1 A.M. three weeks later. Blind Ben commented wryly that carnival duties were an afterthought for most of the troupe. The attention of everyone was focused on the wondrous celebration.

Sharee and Lola were particularly involved in shaping a dress suitable for the occasion from what they had at hand. Their choices were numerous. Twice a day we'd do a "Ladies Only" performance. I had a special spiel:

Every lady on the Midway
Pause for a little lesson
On how to hold your man.
See the latest fashions
from Gay Paree.

Lola modeled see-through nighties and nearly nonexistent undergarments which she sold from a table at the exit. It was obvious that many a farm wife had hidden away a bit of egg money or cash from the sale of cream in order to adorn herself in such a way that her husband would never again need to attend a cooch show.

Sharee modeled exotic formal attire purchased from thrift store racks as we traveled. She carried a sewing machine in her trailer. She had crafted costumes in her college theater troupe.

She was an expert when it came to radically lowering fronts and backs and slitting garments almost to the crotch.

It was Celeste's responsibility to keep up a running dialogue through these presentations. The main point seemed to be that if a woman wearing one of these creations met her man at the door when he came in from the fields for dinner, she'd never have to cook again. His physical needs could be met in a more delightful fashion.

I did have one concern. Every woman I'd ever known wore heavy flannel nighties all winter long. If they donned one of Lola's minuscule offerings, they might freeze to death in their beds.

Preparations reached fever pitch as the wedding day arrived. Ramblin' Rose baked an enormous cake swathed in sugar roses. Guido the Gimp practiced most of the night before illuminating the Fun House platform with a variety of colored lights mounted on the Star of Bethlehem Ferris wheel.

Oscar Sidelka would be Mario's best man. The rest of the dwarf troupe would be flower and ring bearers. Of course, Sharee and Lola would attend Celeste.

I was feeling left out of the formal proceedings. I should be standing at Mario's side. After all, weren't we roommates? Didn't I help him care for his moth-eaten old tiger? He kept commenting mysteriously that I had a special role, which he couldn't tell me about until his wedding night.

As the great day wore on, the odor of the baking wedding cake vied with the earthy smell of creamed onions and boiled cabbage on the regular menu.

The girlie show and the tiger act closed early so that the nuptial pair could ready themselves. When S'tooth had languidly leaped through his hoop one final time, Mario and I stepped into our living quarters.

He stripped off his leopard skin and fright wig. He tossed the caveman's club into a corner and headed for a little trunk standing by his cot. He opened it and took out a set of spangled tights — the same ones he was wearing in the poster.

He called me over as he sat on the cot and asked, "Will you

help me into these, Rog? I'm too twisted to put them on alone."

I stretched the beautiful red fabric over his shattered frame. I helped him into his jeweled slippers. He reached into the trunk and removed an incredibly long golden cape. I snapped it around his shoulders.

He turned to me and, smiling, made an unforgettable request: "When I walk down that Midway with Celeste on my arm, I want you to be my cape bearer."

He furled the cape over his arm. We stepped outside. From every direction carneys were scurrying toward the Fun House. We stopped at Celeste's trailer. Lola and Sharee stepped out first. They were dressed in matching pink sheaths to which modesty had been restored.

Celeste appeared. She was clad in midnight blue. Her face was barely shadowed by a sequined silver veil. Mario handed me the end of the cape and took her hand. We processed down the Midway. Grandma Nell was playing the calliope. The tiny attendants joined us. As we neared the platform, I expected Nell to swing into "Here Comes the Bride." Instead she segued into "The Daring Young Man on the Flying Trapeze." At that, even the toughest carney surreptitiously wiped tears from his or her cheek.

Blind Ben in his preacherly black rose from his gilded throne. The wedding party mounted the platform. Golden light from the Ferris Wheel enveloped them. As they stepped before the Mirror of Truth, Mario unfolded in the reflection. Celeste's perfect features showed through the veil.

Ben said all the usual words. They plighted their troth, and prayers were offered over the rings and they were pronounced husband and wife. Before anyone could applaud or Grandma Nell send them to the reception with calliope melodies, Ben stepped forward, raised his hands for silence and called out, "Guido, put out the lights for a minute."

The area was plunged into darkness. He continued, "I want everyone to look up."

A gasp of wonder rose from those assembled. The aurora

borealis was dancing across the sky. Great sheets of twisted light flared as if flowing from the fingertips of God.

Ben's hushed voice accented the silence: "The wonder of it. The whole universe is at play, and we're all part of the game. Two once-hopeless people now revel in hope, and the heavens laugh with joy. At the heart of it all is love. Just remember that what's happening up there and down here are all one. Each of us is part of the pattern. Amen."

At the end of Ben's words Guido flicked the switch. The platform was flooded with gold. Mario lifted Celeste's veil and kissed her. In the light of the Star of Bethlehem she was incredibly beautiful.

When the ceremony was over, I brushed Celeste's cheek with my lips, furled the cape and hugged Mario as I put it over his arm and melted into the darkness. The crowd was headed for the reception in the cook tent.

When everybody was gone, I returned to the platform and stared at myself in the Mirror of Truth. Though I'd been moved by Blind Ben's words, I saw no dancing heavenly lights shining through from inside me. Would I ever be able to sufficiently cloak my anger to stand with anyone and see us become husband and wife?

I stood there a long time. Guido the Gimp had left the wheel turning. I questioned myself through each of the color changes.

Into the mirror flowed the image of Mario. He said quietly, "I missed you at the party, partner. I thought I knew where I'd find you. What's the trouble?"

I responded, "I'm standing here feeling ugly inside and hopeless in the face of your happiness. All I can hear is the voice of my daddy telling me over and over again, 'You're no damn good.'"

Mario's arm reached up. His assuring hand rested on my shoulder. "It doesn't matter if you're twisted inside or outside or both. Listen deep. You'll hear your own love song one day.

"I've been thinking a lot about those lines you recited to me the night I asked Celeste to marry me. Once in awhile you've got to see yourself as the crooked neighbor. You must love you with all your crooked heart."

He scrabbled down the stairs, turned, grinned up at me and commented wryly, "By the way, don't worry about me, Rog. I have a feeling we're going to mate just fine."

His chuckle echoed over the silent tents. I was glad the light was red at the moment. He couldn't see my blush.

From the edge of light he called back to me, "I love you, Rog."

He disappeared into the darkness.

I headed back toward the tiger van. Mario had moved his spare belongings into Celeste's trailer. I'd sleep alone again.

As I passed the baseball concession, I heard the sound of weeping. Heebee Mazur was standing in a work light, staring at the figure painted on the canvas behind the set bottles. He was juggling two balls in his remaining left hand. His right shoulder twitched strangely as if a phantom arm was striving to join the action.

I momentarily stumbled over a fat electrical cable. Heebee swung around and stared at me. His sobs subsided. The balls remained quiet in his hand. He burst out, "At least Mario is not missing anything. He has two hands to caress her.

"No woman would ever want to spend the night with Heebee, the one-armed freak. Sure, I could tickle her breasts with the hair in the pit of my nonexistent arm. That might turn her on real good. But then she'd have to look at the tangled folds of flesh slopped across my shoulder by a surgeon who never thought I'd make it."

He spun around and threw the balls at the canvas-borne image. He ran off wildly into the night.

The Seashore

There was a long silence. Then Ramblin' Rose sighed, "That was a beautiful scene with you and Mario at the Mirror of Truth, and that was just about the loveliest story I ever heard. And to think, I was even a part of it!"

I responded lightly, "Thank you, madam, for that rare compliment. I'll treasure it always."

She bent over and planted a long kiss on my lips. She said in a playful, sulky voice, "I'd rather you remembered that!"

Ben chuckled: "Rose, you're runnin' off to someone else before my very blinded eyes. Can't never really trust you, can I?"

He enfolded her in a long embrace. The lantern illumined the tenderest of kisses. The old heron standing nearby nodded in approval.

Ben broke away. Turning his sightless eyes on me, he was silent for a long moment. The flame of the lantern reflected from the dark glasses. I was caught in the fire of his insight. He said, "Every story you write strips away a pretense or two about love and about being a person. I sure hope one of these moments you'll hear and believe your own words."

There was an extended silence as I writhed beneath what Ben had snuck in on me. Sensing my discomfiture, Rose said, "I think it's time we got these old bones home."

I helped them to their feet. We gathered up the buffalo hide, blew out the lantern and made our way to the car by the glow of the moon three nights away from full.

As they let me out, Blind Ben queried, "I'm really savorin'

this little expedition into the past. I have only one question: How many more tales are there?"

I hesitated, "Three — I think. I have a feeling there'll be one tomorrow night and two final tales the following night — that is, if my inspiration doesn't flag and your ears and hearts hold up."

Ben retorted, "I have no fear about the former. I worry a bit about the latter. You tacked on a paragraph or two to the story of Mario and Celeste, which leads me to believe I'm being set up for a tough night of facing again the incidents around Heebee Mazur, the baseball player."

I responded, "It'll be tough for me as well. We were sometimes close. I've got to tell his story, and I think you have to listen."

Rose interrupted, "Okay, you two. Quit the philosophizing. After listening to three stories, I need sleep. You need to write, Rog. Go do it!"

As I opened the door to leave, I instructed them, "Don't pick me up anymore. I need the exercise. I'll meet you at the heavenly throne about six."

Ben chuckled, "I think I've just been elevated. Write well, kid, even if the story hurts both me and you."

I watched their headlights disappear.

Just as I was about to step into my seaside shack, the old heron alighted on the roof.

The room was illuminated by the computer monitor. I stripped and stepped into the shower. I let the water run over me until the tiny water heater gave up its largess and freezing water set my every fiber atingle.

I rubbed myself down briskly with the torn towel. I didn't want to go through the pain of writing this story. I reached for my bear and turned the cross so the agonized figure struggling for release was facing out.

I sat at the keyboard. I snuggled the bear into my left armpit. I stared at the screen. Nothing came.

I became aware of a rhythmic tapping on the roof. The

pattern was that which my fingers often took as they flowed across the keyboard. It was Tony, the old heron, doing one of his strange moonlight dances. I let the rhythm grow in me. My fingers began to move. I stumbled bravely into a prologue to the tale.

The Baseball Player

I've got to tell the tale of Heebee Mazur. As you'll soon find out, it could so easily have been my story. You're going to wonder how I discovered some of the details. Well, it happened this way:

Heebee haunted the edge of the group that gathered around Blind Ben See in the wee hours of the morning, the fluorescent eyes on our gold shirts glowing in the flickering rays of the carnival work lights. Sometimes there'd be five or six. Sometimes there'd only be a couple of us. Heebee and I were constants.

I had to be there. I was hanging onto life by my emotional fingernails. If I let go, I'd slide down a long shaft of meaninglessness, accompanied by my mindsick daddy's screams which haunted my dreams every night of my young life.

I would sometimes talk nonstop for a couple hours. Heebee might agonize out a detail or two and then run pell-mell into the darkness. Soon we'd hear the soft "thunk! thunk!" of baseballs striking the bearded face on the tent side.

One night, Heebee ***really*** *talked. We were playing a little town four miles from his father's farm. It was one of those places where people were always making cracks like, "It ain't quite the end of the world, but you can see it from there."*

That night after we finished our setup, Blind Ben held court for just Heebee and me. And Heebee talked. And talked. And talked. He was sitting at Ben's feet. At 3 A.M. he put his head in the old carney's lap and sobbed. Ben embraced him. I gently massaged his neck and shoulders.

Ben spoke to him softly: "I think you can go to your father now, Herbert. I think you've got to go to him. Something like forgiveness has to happen, or your anger will eat your heart out. Go home, Herbert. Know my love and my prayers walk with you."

I knew something special was going on when Blind Ben called Heebee by his rightful name. I watched as the one-armed figure strode off the lot. I was glad he didn't take any of his belongings. It meant he planned to come back. He headed down a country road under the fierce gaze of the morning star.

I heard a sound behind me. Turning around, I found Blind Ben See with his arms resting on his knees. They cradled his bowed head. His body was torn by sobs. I stepped up to him and held him for a long time. He kept muttering, "I don't know what I've done. God, I don't quite know what I've done."

I've never been quite sure if his outcry was a prayer of confession or an expletive.

I headed back to my lonely bed. I wished Mario had been there. I couldn't sleep.

Now, fifteen years later, I try to quilt together a collage of crazy patchwork pieces to cover the grief still aching in a starlit hole in my soul.

Zachariah Mazur rued the day he gave his only child, nine-year-old Herbert Gordon, his first baseball. Heebee, as everybody except his mother, Hannah, called him, slept with the ball under his pillow.

When he was supposed to be weeding the garden, he'd be off in the corner of a vacant pasture throwing the ball in the air and hitting it unexpected distances with a bat which he'd made by sawing a hoe handle in half.

Heebee soon drew the attention of neighbors who would stop their cars on the dusty country road and watch the high-flying ball explode from the makeshift bat.

The next farmer to the north of the Mazurs, Tike Foster, whose son, Randy, had been born on the same day as Heebee, gave Herbert Gordon a real bat on his tenth birthday. Randy had a serious birth injury and would spend the rest of his life in a wheelchair. Tike enjoyed living out the sports-loving piece of himself through the beautifully coordinated neighbor boy.

Zachariah was furious — there was no way he wanted his son to play baseball. He was proud of the fact that his family had homesteaded their three hundred acres in the early 1800s, and as far as he was concerned the farm would be worked by his oldest son according to strict familial tradition.

The Mazur acreage was a showplace. No thistle dared raise its purple head in the fields of lush golden grain. No morning glories wound around the stalks of corn planted in the straightest rows in Buttonwood County. No dandelions marred the lush green lawn which fronted the stark, stolid stone farmhouse.

From the day Heebee emerged from the womb, his father systematically taught his son everything there was to know about farming. As an infant, he was carried to the barn and laid in a manger while Zachariah milked his fourteen cows. Over his wife's objections Zachariah countered roughly, "I just want him to get the feel of the place."

As he grew older, Heebee was taught to maintain the family farm equipment, which was always the latest model. Zachariah's great pride was his hay baler. It could scatter squarely tied bundles of grass over fifty acres in no time flat. Though the Mazurs sometimes skimped on clothing and luxuries, a new baler graced the farm every three years.

Heebee's love of baseball deepened. When he entered junior high, a pattern developed. In fair weather Heebee would get out of bed at 4 A.M., head for the cow barn and begin the milking. When he'd finished his chores, he would slip to the corner of a distant pasture. He'd hit a ball as far as his increasing strength allowed, then run like the wind to retrieve it.

One day Heebee realized he was being observed. He saw a flash of red in the stand of poplars which offered the cattle shade from the summer heat. He walked toward the trees, calling softly, "C'mere, Toby Boy. I won't hurt you. You come on out here."

A skinny ten-year-old with the reddest mop of hair in four counties stepped into the dawn light. Everybody called him by the name his daddy'd given him the first time he held his infant son in his arms. Matt Mertlesen was proud of his beautiful firstborn child. He loved the boy's hair which matched his wife, Merryanne's.

The Mertlesen farm shared the southern boundary of the Mazur place. Whenever extra help was needed for a particular task on any of the three adjoining farms, Zachariah, Matt and Tike Foster would join forces.

Not many months had elapsed after his birth when word went round that "something was wrong" with Toby Boy. He never cried aloud, though tears streamed down his cheeks on occasion. At an age when most little ones were mimicking the sounds of farmyard animals after careful encouragement by proud parents, Toby Boy remained silent. It became evident that Toby Boy was mute.

The Mertlesens took him to specialists at the University of Minnesota and to the Mayo Clinic. Nobody could find a remedy for his speechlessness.

Toby Boy loved the gentle Heebee Mazur. From the time he was old enough to toddle, he followed Heebee around like a little flaming-haired ghost. It was no surprise to find him haunting the poplars on this late spring morning, watching Heebee hit balls.

Toby Boy ran fifty feet in front of Heebee and pantomimed for him to hit a fly ball in his direction. The older boy good-humoredly obliged. The ball arced high against the sunlit sky. Toby Boy stationed himself for its descent and effected a perfect catch. Heebee ran to him and gave him an enormous bear hug.

From that time on the two were together every spare moment. Heebee discovered that his little friend was no slouch when it came to handling a bat and ball. He quickly learned to hit and pitch and could run like a celebrating fawn in pursuit of Heebee's extraordinarily distanced fly balls. As a backstop, they used a great, raven-haunted oak.

One Sunday evening after the three adjoining farm families had spent an afternoon together centered on making a big freezer of ice cream, Zachariah settled into bed next to Hannah and commented, "I watched the boys this afternoon. Randy was turning the crank from his wheelchair. Toby Boy was scrawling notes on that pad of his or acting out what he wanted. I said a little prayer of thanksgiving to Almighty God. Why, just yesterday he plowed the straightest furrow I've ever seen a boy till." Zechariah's face softened as he continued, "It fellt good to walk home with my arm around his shoulders. Yes, Hannah, we got ourselves a perfect son. He'll do this farm proud."

When he entered high school, Heebee's perfection was marred a bit in his father's eyes. He became absolutely focused on baseball. As a sophomore, he became the star of the team. The Oakdale Blazers won the state championship Heebee's first year on the squad. Everybody in baseball circles was talking about Heebee Mazur.

A good deal of his success was due to his red-haired shadow. Heebee'd tell his father that he had a very early morning lab. He'd finish his chores, join up with Toby Boy, and they'd jog the four miles into town. They'd arrive at the deserted school diamond before the sun was up. They'd take turns hitting and pitching.

The town cemetery stood on a little rise beyond the diamond. At dawn, the rounded tombstones looked like hunch-shouldered spectators. Heebee and Toby Boy set a goal of developing their hitting powers so that they could send balls as far as the curlicued wrought iron gate of the burial yard.

One morning Toby Boy nearly exploded with pride when he managed to hit a fly over the cemetery fence. Heebee retrieved it. Handing it back to Toby Boy, he intoned solemnly, "Jeremiah Jenks, born October 4, 1832, died January 8, 1889, thanks you for including him in our game but says it's a bit early in the morning to be waking the dead."

Toby Boy dissolved in silent laughter.

Conflict deepened between Heebee and Zachariah. The boy began to talk about playing college baseball. Scouts spotted him early. There was talk around town that Heebee Mazur might go directly into a professional league. Whenever Zachariah walked the streets of Oakdale, men were always slapping him on the back and congratulating him about his son's latest feat on the diamond. He remained strangely silent.

At home, Zachariah's anger at the prospect of his son disobeying the family's heritage was heaped on Heebee. One evening the elder Mazur sat his son down and without allowing him to respond said, "Everybody's talking about sports scholarships and maybe your playing with the Brooklyn Dodgers. Well, boy, let me get one thing straight with you. Nobody from this family has ever had to go to college. This is the best farm in the area. You can make enough to support a wife and raise a family just like I have.

"No Mazur has ever bummed around the country hitting a ball with a piece of wood."

Hannah tried to intervene, but Zachariah turned on her, shouting, "Shut your damned mouth. This has nothing to do with you. This is between me and my son!"

Turning on Heebee, he continued to shout: "You're not going to start anything new. This farm will be yours someday. You're going to stay right here where you belong and help me work it. Now go to bed!"

Heebee silently left the room, trying to hide his tears.

Toward the end of his senior year, word came out of the principal's office that Herbert Gordon Mazur was the valedictorian of his graduating class. While the rest of the world congratulated him and his mother hugged him in sheer joy, his father remained sullenly silent, fearing the academic achievement might further threaten the possibility of keeping Heebee under his control.

The letter arrived at lunch the day after graduation. Hired hands, in from the hayfield, interrupted their discussion of the virtues of the new baler. Zachariah had shown it off all morning.

Heebee opened the letter. The University of Minnesota was offering him a full athletic scholarship. His shout of joy could be heard across three counties. As his mother put an arm around his shoulder, he exulted, "Even you should be proud of this, Dad."

His father snatched the letter from his hand and shredded it angrily into tiny pieces, shouting, "You're not going nowhere. This farm has been good for Mazurs for over a hundred years, and you-will-not-leave!"

He threw the pieces into the air. They fell like cold snow on Heebee's hopes.

Zachariah dismissed the workmen for the rest of the day, turned on his heel and headed back toward the fields. He paused and tossed placating words to Heebee: "Why don't you run the new baler?"

Heebee pushed past his father and mounted the gleaming green machine. He started it and ground the gears as he whirled angrily out of the yard. His father screamed unheard words of condemnation for his carelessness.

The embittered boy rammed the great machine through the thick alfalfa. He moved too quickly. The mechanism ground to a halt, jammed with an overload of lush vegetation.

A frustrated Heebee leaped from the baler without shifting to neutral. He raged to the rear and began carelessly yanking heavy stems from the yawning maw of the offending implement. When the carrier did not begin moving immediately, he shoved his right arm far into the opening, grasped a handful of course stems and pulled.

The mechanism leaped into action. The descending blades caught Heebee's arm. His screams echoed over the sunlit fields. A flock of crows sailing overhead was riven by the sound. Cawing a discordant dirge of alarm, they settled in the baseball backstop oak which grew at the meeting of fence lines.

With all the strength he could muster, Heebee jerked his arm away from the tearing steel. In his final moment of consciousness he stared at what remained of his right arm: a mangled stump foreshortened to just above where once there had been an elbow. Blood spurted rhythmically to the ground. He collapsed amidst the stubble.

Merryanne Mertlesen had driven her dusty old Ford out into the field to carry lunch to Toby Boy and Matt. The family trio heard Heebee's scream. Merryanne and Matt leaped into the car.

Toby Boy ran like a fear-crazed stallion and opened the gate between the fields. As his mother drove through, Toby Boy leaped onto the running board.

They arrived at the scene of carnage. Merryanne stripped off her apron to shape a tourniquet which she wrapped around the meager arm stump. Matt grabbed a shiny new wrench from the baler tool box. He twirled it in the apron fabric. As it caught the unforgiving sun, it resembled the patterned glow from the baton twirlers with the high school band as they solemnly marched through the cemetery on Memorial Day playing the "Funeral March from 'Aida.'" The chugging baler provided the accompanying bass motif.

Toby Boy knelt in the widening pool of blood, cradling his friend's head in his lap. His falling tears traced rivulets through the dust on Heebee's face.

The blood flow diminished to a gentle ooze.

"We've got to get him to the hospital right away," said Matt.

The three of them lifted Heebee gently into the car. Toby Boy continued to hold his friend.

Merryanne slipped behind the wheel. As Matt ran around the car to the passenger side, he paused to turn off the baler engine. A wave of nausea nearly overcame him as he noticed a bloody bale emerging from the machine. A shred of Heebee's shirtsleeve was caught in the encasing twine. It flowed in the soft summer breeze like a warning flag.

Swallowing hard, he leaped into the car. They drove quickly to the Oakdale hospital. Heebee was rushed into surgery.

Merryanne called Hannah Mazur. Zachariah was "off somewhere in the car." Merryanne drove into the country to carry the sobbing woman to her son's side.

The prognosis was as good as it could be. Heebee would live. However, the surgeon had to remove the remainder of the limb cleanly at his shoulder.

Merryanne returned Hannah to the farm mid-evening. They were met at the door by a raging Zachariah, who expostulated, "I had to drive fifty miles to find a tractor part, and I arrived home expecting dinner on the table. I found myself deserted by my worthless wife and worthless son, and I had to gnaw on cold chicken and applesauce!"

Hannah began to sob.

Peppery Merryanne stepped up to the bearded patriarchal figure and shouted, "Shut up for a moment, Zachariah. Let me try to make you understand what's happened."

She outlined the events surrounding the accident. Zachariah was silent for a moment. Then he breathed out, "Praise be to God. Praise be to God. It's the will of the Father. The stupid boy was determined to leave his heritage. God has intervened."

He paused for a moment, then ground out through clenched teeth, "Now-he'll-stay."

As she stepped closer to confront the grim-faced man, Merryanne exploded, "You self-centered sonofabitch!"

She slapped him resoundingly across the face, then fled from the room. A quick smile flowed through Hannah's tears as the slam of the screen door shattered the silence of the star-studded night.

Zachariah slumped to his chair at the kitchen table and fiddled with a gnawed bone. Without a word, Hannah stepped stolidly to the kitchen stove. She stole a glance at her husband's face illumined by the soft light from the kerosene sconce lamp glowing before its brightly polished reflector shield. The fiery red marks of Merryanne's fingers flamed on his impassive face.

Hannah lighted dry corncobs in the cast-iron stove. Tears melted down her waxlike face and sizzled softly as the fire caught. In a few minutes she placed before her silent husband a plate of fried potatoes laced with bacon and topped with three eggs, sunny-side up. She added a side of warmed-up biscuits, a cup of strong coffee and a piece of apple pie.

She slipped into the bedroom and collapsed, not worrying that the fresh flow of her tears might stain her newly quilted Sunflower Sue coverlet.

The party line telephone enabled news of Heebee's tragedy to spread through the neighborhood. There was a knock at the Mazurs' door. Zachariah rose slowly from his repast to open the screen. It was Tike Foster and his wife, Maddie. She pushed past the grim-faced man and followed the sound of Hannah's dirge-like wailing.

Tike held out his hand, saying, "I was real sorry to hear about Heebee's tragedy. He's always been a brother to Randy. He never makes fun of him in his wheelchair."

Since the proffered hand went unacknowledged, Tike shoved it into the pocket of his faded overalls. He continued, "Matt Mertlesen called me. He says we ought to retrieve the baler and when we do, we should take a couple of shovels with us."

Zachariah spoke for the first time: "Yes. We've got to get my new baler into the machine shed before dewfall. I wouldn't want it to rust."

Tike stepped to the toolshed and picked up shovels. The men walked across the field. A bloated, blooded harvest moon was lifting itself languidly from the eastern horizon. Against it stood the stark outline of the offending machine.

Zachariah patted it gently, climbed to the operator's seat and started the engine. Its roar stunned the starlit silence. Tike stood at the end of the conveyor to receive the funereal bale. As it slid to the ground, he saw the shredded bit of shirtsleeve.

Tike stepped to the twine feeder and cut two lengths. He quickly attached a handle to either end of the bale. The men carried it across the field. Beneath the crow dappled oak they dug a grave and buried the bloodstained relic of human anger. As they turned to leave, the moon had risen high, its bloodied face now a clean, piercing yellow. Its light caressed the lonely grave.

Toby Boy never left Heebee's bedside the two weeks he was hospitalized. Zachariah refused to visit his son. He was not about to "baby him" by exhibiting any softness related to his foolish accident. Merryanne delivered Hannah to the hospital each day. She met her up the road from the Mazur farmstead, not wanting any further confrontations with the bearded fury.

Tike Foster brought a wan, heavily bandaged Heebee home two weeks to the day from the accident. Zachariah was away in a distant field.

He came in late from plowing corn. Hannah and Heebee were sitting at the kitchen table having supper. His mother had carefully cut up his favorite rare steak, determined to "get a little meat on his bones." He was fumbling as he ate, trying to manipulate fork and spoon with his left hand.

His father sat down silently and stared at his mangled son. Hannah quickly rose and removed Zachariah's meal from the warming oven. He deftly carved his beef and potatoes. Heebee helplessly looked on.

Finally, Zachariah spoke: "I've just been figuring. There's lots of things a one-armed man can do on a farm."

Heebee stumbled from the table, his left hand balled in a tight fist. He paused as if prepared to strike his smug-faced father. Instead, he lashed out at the kitchen door. His fist went straight through the flimsy screen. He kicked it open and fled into the gathering dusk. The discordant slam of the battered door was quickly followed by the strained sounds of Heebee retching in the rose garden.

His mother wilted into her arms on the kitchen table. His father calmly finished his dinner.

The next two months Heebee spent most of his time on his knees, crawling through extensive potato fields, pulling pigweeds and knocking shiny brown marauding bugs into a small can of kerosene. This task was usually given to children and incompetents. The fact that his father assigned him the most humiliating job on the farm was not lost on Heebee.

One late August night Toby Boy met Heebee in their favorite place: mid-field between their farms under the great oak tree. Heebee assured his friend, "I sometimes like to visit the rest of me."

In the distance they could see the revolving lights of the Star of Bethlehem Ferris wheel. Calliope music drifted over the harvested fields of alfalfa, oats and barley. Blind Ben See's Carnival of Wonders was making its yearly pilgrimage to Oakdale.

Heebee said quietly, "I've packed up a few things. I'm going to slip away tonight and join the carnival. I've told Ma. I never want my father to know where I am the rest of my life.

"I want you to have all my baseball stuff. You're an even better player than I was at your age. Toby Boy, you can be the best high school baseball player in the state — just like me."

Toby Boy's bright red hair flamed in the moonlight as he threw his arms around Heebee. They hugged and then set off in opposite directions.

Later that night a shadowy figure with a small valise in its left hand scurried across the fields toward Oakdale, where Scartown was tearing down in preparation for moving on.

That's how the carnival acquired the moody man who ran the baseball concession.

It was early in the morning after Ben had encouraged Heebee to reconcile with his father. I accompanied the old blind man to the cook tent. We didn't speak about the baseball player. In my heart I knew both of us hungered for a full report.

We spotted the gaily festooned truck of Teddy Tomlinson. The signs encouraged the world to buy Wonder Bread. Teddy was always glad when the show came to town. Carneys have bottomless pits for stomachs. His business tripled for the month.

He was a balding bachelor who talked nonstop whenever he emerged from his solitary dwelling. He fancied Ramblin' Rose's French toast which she always served the first morning in Oakdale. Ben invited him to stay for breakfast. Year after year the lonely man tried to convince Rose to settle down in his quiet town.

Lola thought he was cute. However, when that statuesque lady began to move toward him, a welcoming smile on her face, the little man fled.

This morning he joined Blind Ben and me. We were the only occupants of the tent since the sun was scarcely up. Teddy put his plate on the table. It was graced with six slices of Rose's vanilla-flavored delicacy buried in melted butter and powdered sugar.

He began chattering immediately: "I feel like I've put in a whole day's work, what with the terrible thing that's happened and all. The party line started humming at 4 A.M. Zachariah Mazur called Matt Mertlesen, who called Tike Turner. All that phoning so early in the morning got everybody out of bed to listen in on the party line. With all that rubbernecking, news travels real fast in these parts. Most folks threw on some clothes and got to the Mazur place as soon as they could.

"Whenever there's an awful tragedy of some kind, I always stop by and drop off a half a dozen loaves of bread and a few rolls, compliments of the company, 'cause we know there's going to need to be lots of sandwiches made."

I looked at Ben with a sinking heart. His face was ashen. He inquired haltingly, "What happened at the Mazur place?"

Teddy was only too glad to be the initial bearer of bad news: "It's terrible. Just terrible. Real early this morning Zachariah Mazur was heading for the barn. The old yellow farm dog was whining at the machine shed door. Suspecting a raccoon or skunk might have gotten in, Zachariah opened the door, and there, hanging from a rafter right over his new hay baler, was the body of that one-armed boy of his who used to play baseball.

"He'd taken a rope of braided baler twine which Hannah had just finished so Zachariah could repair his hay sling. He'd put the heavy wooden orchard ladder against a rafter, climbed up and kicked the ladder away. It crashed into the new baler and made a huge dent in it. Zachariah told Matt Mertlesen that if the boy had to destroy hisself, why in hell did he have to damage something else at the same time?"

My gut clutched and my neck itched as memories of standing those hours with a rope at ready crashed in upon me. I'd been enveloped in despair that was driving me to almost be as Heebee now was.

Teddy had not paused in his narration: "When Matt and Tike Foster arrived to help get the body down, Zachariah had them move the machine so that just in case the body dropped it wouldn't put another ding in its brightly polished surface.

"They got him down okay. Hannah just about went crazy with grief. The only comfort Zachariah could offer was quoting the Bible at her. He kept repeating Hebrews 12, 6: 'For whom the Lord loveth he chasteneth, and scourgeth every son whom he receiveth.'

"Hannah went home with Merryanne Mertlesen. There's some question in folk's mind whether or not she'll ever go back. If Merryanne has anything to say about it, she won't. There's no love lost between her and old man Mazur.

"The funeral's tomorrow at 2 P.M. in Loving Savior Lutheran Church. We don't usually put people away that fast in Oakdale, but Zachariah wants it done as quick as possible. He says there's no point in stopping the whole world for any longer than necessary just because of the foolishness of man.

"Pertie Fluellen, who owns the Coast to Coast hardware and undertaking establishment, says he'll have to work like the blazes to get Heebee ready for viewing by 5 o'clock. The twine rope tore him up pretty bad. Everybody in town's going to want to pay their respects.

"And there may be some problem at the church. We got ourselves a new pastor name of Bartholomew Brittleheimer. He's some preacher. His sermons will scare the hell out of you, if you take my meaning. He's pretty Bible-centered and says Heebee committed two mortal sins: not honoring his father and killing himself. He doesn't really think the service should be in the church and that Heebee ought to be buried outside the walls of the regular cemetery as an example to anybody tempted to do the same terrible thing he did.

"However, Zachariah talked to him. The pastor finally agreed to do it in the church for the family and a few close friends, and Heebee could be buried in the Mazur plot. Most everybody thought the new preacher would come around since old man Mazur pledges more money to the church budget than anybody else. Most folk think Hannah will sit with her husband tomorrow just to keep up appearances.

"I'm here to tell you, I've never known of an event that got the whole town so riled up. Ellie Schlingenhagel opened the Bus Stop Grill two hours early just so folks had some place to get a cup of coffee and talk about it all. You'd be surprised how many are seeing themselves as close family friends just so they can go to the service.

"Toby Boy Mertlesen and his folks came by the Bus Stop. The kid wrote something on the back of a menu about burying Heebee under some tree in some field where his arm already was, but most folk thought that would be real odd, and old man Mazur would never stand for it in a hundred years.

"Tike Foster came into the cafe and reported that about midnight Randy had had some kind of an attack or other. He'd rushed him into town. The doc took care of him real fast. On their way home about three in the morning, Tike said they'd passed the Mazur place. They were driving with the car windows down. Zachariah and Heebee had been standing out in the yard screaming at one another. Tike feels real bad, now, that he never stopped, but folks around here respects one another's privacy.

"Well, now that I've given you all the most important news from town, I'd better be gettin' back. By this time Ellie'll prob'ly be out of everything at the Bus Stop."

He leaped to his feet and shouted, "Thanks for the French toast, Rose. It was scrumptious."

He quickly disappeared. I looked at his plate. I was dumbfounded. He'd managed to consume six slices while seldom taking a breath during his nonstop narrative. I was going to suggest to Blind Ben that he open another side show and call it the Amazing Digestive Man.

As I turned my attention from Teddy's plate to the old man, I found him collapsed on the rough table, his body shaken by sobs. I rushed around and cradled him in my arms.

He kept whispering over and over again, "I encouraged risk, and we all lost. I encouraged risk, and we all lost."

Ramblin' Rose had disappeared to spread the news. The tent began to fill. Tears streamed down the cheeks of everybody. The Scartown family gathered around Ben and me in concentric circles of hugging. The eyes on their golden shirts were moist even though it was too early in the day for anyone to work up a sweat.

Ben shook himself free of my arms. Bracing his hand on my shoulder, he climbed on the bench. I kept an arm around his waist. Sharee pushed forward and held his left hand against her cheek. Alligator Al held his right.

He addressed his assembled family. Words stumbled out through his sobs: "I've got a confession to make. Late last night I encouraged Heebee to go and reconcile with his daddy. He was so torn up by grief and anger he couldn't go on living with himself here or anywhere else.

"None of us agree with the route he took to get beyond his pain, but none of us can condemn him. I call this show my Carnival of Wonders. The real wonder is that any of us can survive what most of us have been through. We make a place of refuge for each other. Sometimes folks don't see that place as wide enough to hold a particular grief.

"Right now we're all embracing each other. In our grief we're more *family* than we've ever been. I hope each of you in this tent remembers this moment the rest of your life so that when you walk to the edge of despair you recall this saving moment. Remember that there is love available to heal you if you open yourself wide enough to find it. Heebee chose to grovel in his anger, and it led him to the rope."

I winced. I had done a lot of anger-groveling in my time.

Blind Ben See continued, "We'll run the show today. Tomorrow we'll keep it closed and all go into Oakdale for Heebee's service. Does anybody have anything black they could drape over the baseball concession?"

The dwarf troupe stepped forward and said they'd take care of it, but they'd need a little help mounting whatever they created. I volunteered.

Ben concluded: "I think we should spend a little time praying. I want to start with some quiet so each of you can remember Heebee in your own way."

A beautiful silence settled over the tent. Everybody was in touch with everybody else and with Something beyond themselves. After a few minutes, Ben prayed, "O God, Herbert Gordon Mazur has bulldozed his way through the gates of paradise. Open your arms to him with your eternal hug. Amen."

The carnival folk sat down around the tables, quietly talking. Camille, who juggled with the dwarf troupe, climbed up on a stool behind the counter and helped Rose flip French toast.

I couldn't eat. I was drawn to the baseball tent. The sullen, bearded face painted on the canvas was illumined by a ray of early morning sun. For a moment the beard disappeared in my mind, and there was the face of my mindsick daddy. I wondered if all abusive daddies looked something alike.

I picked up a ball and sent it crashing into the portrait. Though tears distorted my aim, I flung ball after ball after ball with wild abandon until my supply and my arm were both exhausted. I sank to the ground.

A tiny hand ran through my hair and softly stroked the tears from my cheek. It was Rix. The dwarf troupe had arrived. They carried a long piece of black crepe which they'd planned to use in a Tom Thumb funeral to balance off the wedding but decided it might be too morbid for the audience.

Mick and Dan, the contortionists, held the cloth while Glenilda pinned tiny artificial roses in the shape of letters, which finally read, "For Heebee With Love." I was tall enough to reach the corners of the booth and artfully drape the handiwork under the directorial eye of Rix.

The following morning it was decided that the carnival troupe would walk in procession to the service. The carousel led the way. Grandma Nell played "When the Roll Is Called Up Yonder, I'll Be There," "Rock of Ages" and "The Old Rugged Cross." Blind Ben and I followed the music. The rest of the company trailed out behind for about three blocks.

The dancers wore matching black sheaths. I was pleased with Celeste. She wore no veil. The longer she was married to Mario, the less ashamed she was of her scars. If people couldn't see beneath them to her inherent grace, that was their problem.

In the distance we spotted the squat, severe spire of Loving Savior Lutheran Church topped by a lightning-twisted cross. I knew that above the merry sound of the calliope we should by this time have heard the tolling of the tower bell. Anybody who died got at least that much public affirmation. Grandma Nell paused for a moment between selections. The bell was mute. She resumed pealing out great arpeggios of praise to the Creator of life and death and life again.

As we neared the imposing edifice, the front door burst open. We were confronted by the enormous figure of Pastor Bartholomew Brittleheimer, his somber robes ballooning out in the hot summer wind.

Patmandi, the Snake Charmer whispered to Floy, the Fat Lady, "Look, Floy. At last we've found someone who nearly approaches your fine stature. Maybe he could become interested in you."

"Sorry, Pat." she shot back. "I don't want to marry beneath me."

We approached the bottom of a long flight of steps leading up to the sanctuary door. A sound resembling the bellow of an outraged rutting bull frustrated in his quest flared down upon us. Within the bluster, an occasional word could be discerned: "Stop! You will not enter this sacred space. I now understand why the deceased violated the laws of heaven. It comes from living among Satan's scum: thieves, vagabonds and destroyers of the bond of holy wedlock."

The dancers glanced at each other with wry smiles. Celeste squeezed Mario's hand a little tighter.

The pastor had a great voice. I could quickly teach him to be a fine carnival spieler. I thought for a moment and decided that's what he really was now.

During Brittleheimer's outburst, Ben slowly, deliberately mounted the steps, the sunlight glinting harshly from his dark glasses. One step beneath him on either side processed Alligator Al and Oscar Sidelka. They reflected the pattern of the triangular symbol for the Trinity carved above the church door. I giggled as I momentarily wondered which of the carneys was the Father, which was the Son and which was the Holy Ghost.

Blind Ben spoke quietly, his voice carrying steel-edged determination: "Calm yourself, brother. I understand your trouble. I was a pastor once myself, trying to protect my private bit of holy turf. Let me assure you we come in love. We've been the only family Herbert Gordon Mazur has known for the past two years."

Ben's voice broke as he continued, "He's been like a son to me."

He looked over his shoulder at the denizens of Scartown spread out behind him and said, "They're my family. All we ask is to be allowed in Christ's church for Heebee's memorial moments."

The robed mountain of a man blustered on, "The men of my congregation will never allow this church to be soiled by such as you!"

Blind Ben performed his ultimate act. He slowly stepped up within three feet of the false prophet fulminating before him and removed his dark glasses. The festering pits seemed to ooze with particular malevolence.

Pastor Brittleheimer's scream could be heard in the next county. He fled through the imposing doors carved with the figure of Jesus ascending to heaven on a cloud. The words above him read, "Go ye into all the world."

Blind Ben returned his glasses to his nose, turned and beckoned us all to follow. As we entered the church, I caught a glimpse of people scurrying from the rear pews where they comfortably reclined on Sunday morning to the front so that the carneys would be segregated in the back where they belonged.

We settled into our proper places. I carry in my heart four images from that service: the tearless face of Zachariah Mazur, the rabid stream of condemnation that poured from the preacher's lips, the shock of unruly red hair on the teenager torn by silent sobs sitting closest to the cheap pasteboard pauper's casket in which the angry old man had chosen to lay his son away (the youngster had to be Heebee's beloved, wordless Toby Boy) and the great stained glass window which fronted the sanctuary. Jesus was pictured standing chastely clothed in the Jordan river. John the Baptist poured a shell full of water over his head. An intensely white, well-rounded dove was captured mid-flight descending in the center of the glass. A burst of lightning emanated from the top, projecting the words, "This is my beloved Son in whom I am well pleased."

There was no organ music in the service. No hymns were sung. Only words of condemnation and warning shattered the stillness of the sanctuary. I kept wishing Grandma Nell would slip out and play the calliope in the background.

When the preacher had exhausted himself and us, he came down from the high pulpit and stood protectively at the foot of the coffin. We were invited to pass by and view what well could be the conclusion of our sinning if we didn't turn to Jesus. A contradictory thought crossed my mind. Tony Great Turtle had always assured me that I was going to die, so I shouldn't shadow present moments with hurtful things. Now, I had just sat through an hour of terrible pain in the shadow of death.

Toby Boy was the first to pause. He carried a brand new baseball. He reached into the casket and gently balanced the gleaming white orb on the curved thumb and forefinger of Heebee's left hand which was resting on his motionless chest. The obese pastor moved to the center with amazing agility, grabbed the offending ball and shoved it back into Toby Boy's hand.

I brought up the end of the line. As we neared the casket, I could see that Zachariah had clothed his son in a new black suit. It further disguised who Heebee really was to "keep up appearances."

Blind Ben was just ahead of me. He paused by Heebee. He touched his own lips with the index finger of his left hand and traced the sign of the cross on his surrogate son's forehead. He reached inside his coat and pulled out a golden shirt. The fluorescent eye was dimmed with grief. Ben spread it carefully over Heebee's chest. He even managed to work it under the left hand.

The Reverend Brittleheimer leaped forward again. Randy

Mertlesen shot out of the aisle in his wheelchair and blocked the charging preacher, running over Pastor Bartholomew's foot in the process. Simultaneously, Ben turned on him, his right hand heading for his glasses. The cleric gasped and retreated.

Undertaker Fluellen rushed up and gingerly closed the lid so as not to snap off the cheap tin latch.

We all walked in procession to Heebee's grave. His pall-bearers were members of the present high school baseball team for whom he'd been a hero as they grew up. They all wore their purple player's caps with golden "O's" emblazoned on the beaks. Toby Boy led the way behind the waddling figure of the profusely sweating minister.

We gathered around the grave. More grim words were spoken. The requisite handful of dirt was tossed on the coffin. The service snaked its way to an abrupt conclusion. The pastor quickly left as if remaining would violate his real feelings about the situation. I momentarily pitied him.

Folks faded away to their distant cars.

I'd heard talk that the grave wouldn't be filled in right away. Riley Roberson, who pumped gas at the Texaco station, doubled as cemetery attendant. He'd just gotten word that his four-year-old daughter, Emerald Jean, had fallen out of a tree and broken her arm. He sent word back that he was not about to desert his lively daughter in order to care for the dead. He'd be back in the evening to finish off his grave work.

I told Ben I couldn't leave Heebee alone. The rest of the carneys headed for the lot, silent except for Grandma Nell's calliope theme and variations on "Bringing in the Sheaves." As the troupe moved through the cemetery gates and on down the street, she segued into "Blue Skies Smilin' at Me." The last two lines of the song would not be a bad epitaph:

> Blue days, all of them gone;
> Nothin' but blue skies, from now on.

I sat by the open pit and watched a magnificent sunset whirl into place, the wind skittering wisps of clouds across the fiery golden sky.

Suddenly, I was aware of movement centered on a flash of flaming red — not in the transformed heavens but on home plate of the high school baseball diamond.

It was Toby Boy with a bat over his shoulder and the ball which Brittleheimer had rejected bouncing up and down from his left hand. He paused and measured a particular distance with a practiced eye.

He tossed the ball in the air and gave it a mighty whack. The crack of the bat echoed into the approaching twilight. The gleaming ball arced high into the flaming sky. Then, like a snow-white dove, it descended directly into Heebee's open grave.

The hurtling orb exploded the flimsy lid. I peered into the gathered dusk in the bottom of the grave. The ball was balanced perfectly on Heebee's thumb and forefinger. The eye on the golden shirt winked in satisfaction.

Within the ear of my heart I heard the words, "This is my beloved son in whom I am well pleased."

The Seashore

I was jarred awake by the sound of a beak tolling against the window like a monastery matins bell. The old blue heron was demanding sustenance in return for inspiration.

I stumbled to my feet and returned my bear to its place of honor while avoiding the eyes of the grimacing Christ. I retrieved some shrimp from the freezer, opened the door and let Tony eat them from my hand. With a studied delicacy he nibbled them up. His beak tickled my palm. I laughed aloud, letting the dark vapor of the story disappear in the morning mist rising from the sea.

I had alternately written and dozed through the night. I glanced over my shoulder. The final lines of affirmation glowed on the screen. In celebration I raced across the narrow stretch of sand and threw myself into the advancing tide.

I swam hard, then floated lazily on my back. I was exhausted. I was down to my last two stories — in many ways the hardest of the lot. I knew if I wrote them, I'd have to give something up — maybe even give up my self-destructive anger at my father. I wasn't ready to do that. It had been with me all my life. If I resolved it, would there be anything left that was really me?

I was jarred back to the present by the thrust of the incoming tide scraping my bare butt across the shell beds in the shallows. I struggled to my feet. A wave snuck up behind me and knocked me flat. The lone heron looked on in wry amusement as I emerged battered by the sea.

I entered the shack.

Images from the two final tales tantalized me. I did not want to deal with them. I had to — but not now. I remembered a line I'd once performed in a play: "We desire to escape into sleep from that which we do not understand." I moved across the room and set the computer to "print."

Not even the clatter of the old printer could hold back my slumber.

I wakened with a start almost twelve hours later. It was nearly five. I pulled on my Speedo cutoffs and my mystic shirt, tore off the latest manuscript pages and jogged up the beach. I arrived at an empty throne.

Settling down in the sand at its foot, I stared out over the sea. Pelicans skimmed small fish. Sandpipers inserted pin-like beaks into tiny cochinas. I was ringed by gulls expecting me to be a major food source. Stars appeared. Suddenly the buffalo robe descended over my head, and Ramblin' Rose collapsed on top of me, shouting, "Surprise!"

She and Ben were engulfed in laughter. He knelt in the sand. I disengaged myself and wrapped the robe around the two of them. I lighted the Coleman lantern and moved to Ben's side so, if need be, I could put an arm around him as I read. I started "The Baseball Player."

When I got to the part about Heebee's body being discovered in the machine shed, Ben shook with dry sobs. They quieted as I described the prelude to the funeral. Ramblin' Rose broke into gales of laughter. The sea wind must have carried the sound as far as my shack, for the old heron appeared and circled quizzically above us.

At the final line they were both crying softly.

Ben muttered, "I couldn't believe it — that any father would so completely wall off the love created in him. Your father, Rog — him I could understand, since he was sick in his mind. In Zachariah Mazur's case, it was sheer, destructive, petulant control. I couldn't believe it: I sent Heebee to his death."

It was my turn to do a bit of clarification: "Ben, you are wrongly assuming responsibility for that over which you had absolutely no control. I've heard you say on occasion how an essential part of our gift from the Creator is choice-making. We make dumb choices, but they're ours. To deny that fact is to deny something of our sacredness.

"Ben, Heebee made a choice in anger and despair. Strangely, it was part of his gift — part of his sacredness, even if it violated a lot of sensitivities.

"Had I stepped through the trapdoor when I was fourteen, I would have hurt a lot of people, but it would have been my decision. I didn't have to respond to Hillis' call.

"I know you don't condemn Heebee. At the same time, don't condemn yourself. In the act of self-condemnation you put yourself in the Olympian position of ultimate control. Leave that to God."

Blind Ben See was silent for a moment. Rose was about to insert a comment. I put my finger across her lips.

Ben broke the stillness with a gale of laughter and choked out, "Well, the pupil is usurping the place of the master. That was purposeful pontificating, boy. I may even believe some of it after I ponder for a while.

"You know, I never had any children. You and Heebee and Mario were my kids. One always hates to lose a youngster — but if we ask too many questions, we dig a pit for ourselves. I'm glad we listened to your reading on a night like this with the moon close to full and a million stars — and that great, strange bird circling up there. It puts everything in a slightly different perspective."

Rose began struggling to her feet. She was getting more and more feeble, but she'd never admit it in a thousand years.

She commented, "Wow! That was something, kid — to live through all those moments one more time. But I've had sufficient entertainment for the evening. We'll just shove you down the beach and meet you here same time tomorrow night for what I expect will be the final installment. Time to say good night, kid."

I helped Ben to his feet. I put my arms around them both and said quietly, "I hope you two realize just how much I love you."

Rose countered, "I sort of guessed it, but it sure has taken a long time for you to come right out and say it. Now, walk us to the car and git yer butt down to the beach home and git to writin'. I happen to know you've got to write one last story about Sharee."

I interrupted, "Yes — but there's one story beyond it in which you two play no role. I'll leave it at that for now. There'll be an element of surprise."

We reached the car. They climbed stiffly into their seats. Rose called out through the window, "I'm sorry we're comin' to the end. This has been kinda' fun — tears and all."

The headlights disappeared.

I strolled down the beach. The old heron walked near me at the edge of the water alternately picking an occasional morsel from beneath the surface and looking at me anxiously. He seemed to sense the pain building up inside, ready to explode on the page.

I rushed into the shack. The heron remained at the window. Stripping, I paused for neither shower nor salt swim. I sat down at the computer after flipping the crucifix to triumph. That's where I hoped I'd end up when I finished the two final stories, which I had to write as one.

Words flowed in a steady stream across the screen straight from my heart's memory.

The Desecration of Sharee

The little towns we played in southern Minnesota and northern Iowa considered themselves good Christian villages. They reluctantly allowed the carnival to enter their sacred precincts. Yet they did open their doors. After all, some of the proceeds went into the town coffers or benefited the Elks or Rotarians, who often sponsored our appearances.

An occasional site would not allow the seductive presence of "Ze Bra." In such cases, a bargaining chip was often proffered. If one of the dancers would spend a few private hours with the mayor or the chief of police after the show closed for the night, we could open the cooch tent.

Sharee and Lola were supposed to alternate in this distasteful task, but Lola went most often. I'd hear them laughing together the morning after as Lola would relate how her presence so overpowered her prospective lover that he never got around to taking off his clothes. She sat for three hours listening to him narrate the inadequacies of his wife and watching him drink himself into stupidity.

As we approached Bingham's Meadow in northern Iowa, word came down that the moral gates of the town were closed to "Ze Bra" unless Sharee herself would spend the wee hours of the morning with a city father.

The specific request made me uncomfortable. I was even

more fearful when the hawk-nosed man in the gray flannel suit appeared for four of our six performances. In the harsh light of high noon he resembled my mindsick daddy so completely that my tongue stumbled over my spiels.

Between shows, I shared my uneasiness with Sharee. She laughed lightly and said, "I've been practicing Lola's techniques of male intimidation. We girls really do know how to take care of ourselves."

That night as the show closed I pleaded with Sharee not to go. She said gently, "It's okay, Rog. This is part of our making a living. I appreciate your concern. I've always said you're just about the politest man I've ever met."

She embraced me warmly. Quick and chaste as it was, it ranked right up there in importance with the hugs of Gletha the Goatlady and my Hermit Uncle John.

The pickup point on such occasions was the work light in the parking area nearest the jungle van. I headed for the lot just before 1 A.M. and sat in the soft gravel at the base of the light, leaning against the pole.

Sharee appeared in the distance. Before she could reach me, a long gray Lincoln crawled into the parking lot. It paused at her side. She got in.

The vehicle spun away. As it passed, flying gravel stung my cheeks. I caught a quick glimpse of the driver. My heart plunged. It was the hawk-nosed man in the gray flannel suit. In that fleeting instant, he looked more like my daddy than ever before.

I did not move from my vigil point. Time crept by. I whirled in a waking nightmare. Every incident of abuse inflicted on me by my mindsick father regurgitated out of my subconscious. My buttocks stung from nine willow branch slashes. My left instep ached from his hobnailed boot crashing down on it. My wrists and shoulders remembered the terror of being hung on the horse stall wall. My groin flamed with pain from his brutal raping thrusts.

I sobbed until my tears were gone. My body was torn by dry heaves. I wanted to seek out Mario or Blind Ben or Ramblin' Rose. I couldn't pull myself away from my watch post, nor was

I sure I had the strength to stumble through the silent trailers to a place of refuge.

It was nearly 4 A.M. I heard the roar of an engine echoing across the countryside. I struggled to my feet. A car's lights careened from side to side on the narrow road like a crazed pinball machine.

The long gray Lincoln whirled crazily into the lot and headed straight for me. I leaped out of the way. The driver slammed on his brakes scarring the surface of the ground with a jagged furrow as the car's rear end whiplashed in the loose gravel.

The hawk-nosed man reached across Sharee. He opened the passenger side door, grabbed her by the shoulder and roughly ejected her. She staggered, tried to keep her balance, then slowly wilted to the ground.

The driver slammed the open door. He spun the car around. He was headed directly for Sharee's motionless body. He paused as if considering whether or not to run her over. He drew alongside her, paused and violently started again. As the rear wheels spun, dirt desecrated the fallen victim's motionless form. He bulleted out of the lot and feverishly wove down the quiet road past cows sleeping peacefully in the starlight.

I rushed to Sharee and knelt at her side.

She was half naked. Bits of clothing including a golden carnival T-shirt were shredded. Her face was swollen almost beyond recognition. Her entire body was dappled by bruises. She was unconscious.

I ran for Lola. She sleepily opened her trailer door, but she became completely alert as I quickly shared Sharee's condition.

She leaped down the steps in her skimpy nightgown. She called over her shoulder, "Fetch Celeste and Mario. Get Blind Ben. Stop and have Ramblin' Rose bring ice from her cooler and a stack of towels."

I ran like the wind, almost knocking Blind Ben over as he came around a corner. His inner eye had sensed disaster somehow related to "Ze Bra."

Soon Sharee was surrounded by sentinels of caring. Gently, we picked her up and carried her to her book-lined trailer.

The women sponged the dirt from wounds. She reeked with the rank, unmistakable odor of semen.

I ran to the cook tent to help Ramblin' Rose. She'd filled a bucket with ice. I carried it while she picked up an armload of soft white Turkish towels.

As we entered, Sharee began to moan aloud and move a bit. We all began folding ice into towels. Mario and Blind Ben laid them on the worst of the bruises. As I handed them ice packs, I noticed the soft, lacerated skin on her ankles and wrists. My own wrists from which my daddy'd hanged me years ago flamed into pain as I recalled the fresh hemp rope he'd used. My flesh had been needled until the blood ran down my outstretched arms.

Sharee opened her eyes. Blind Ben was leading us in prayer for her healing. Scattered phrases of terror tore themselves from her, interwoven with the sacred supplications.

"Healing One, dwell now in this humble, hurting place . . . *cabin . . . so dark . . . on lake* . . . bring light to our sister's darkness . . . *he said nothing during drive* . . . may we hear within our silent terror thy holy voice . . . *smelled of booze in the silence* . . . let the incense of thy love so fill Sharee that she need never be afraid again . . . *stepped from car into darkness shot through with loon calls* . . . . Open the ears of her heart so that she may be gifted by thy voice in unexpected moments . . . *wished for starlight . . . hungered for moonlight* . . . . May the beams of blessedness shine on this wounded sister and give her peace. Amen.

I was glad for the loon calls in the distance. Gletha the Goatlady had always made me hear within them the voice of God. She said the Holy One wouldn't take away my daddy's sickness but would only walk with me through the horror, giving me strength to bear it by gifting me with sacred sounds like calls of the wolf, the owl and the loon.

Mario and I each held one of Sharee's hands. Blind Ben gently stroked his index finger across her forehead, avoiding an ugly swelling on her temple which made her wince when he first touched it.

She struggled to share her story as if in the process she could knock the edge off her terror and disgust: "He grabbed me as I stepped from the car. He crushed me in his arms and bruised my lips with his teeth as he kissed me, ramming his tongue down my throat.

"He dragged me inside a tumble-down cabin. It was littered with beer bottles and smelled like a brewery. A single kerosene wall lamp flickered in front of a filthy reflector.

"The door to an inner room burst open. Four naked men tumbled out, yelling, 'Surprise!' like children at a birthday party. While my captor stripped, they shoved me from one to another as each tore off a piece of my clothing.

"They slapped me, punched me and shouted obscenities. There seemed to be a single theme in their rambling rage: I was a slut of Satan because I danced in the carnival, causing men to have evil thoughts, making them leave their wives. I destroyed homes and orphaned children. So, it was their Christian duty to use the 'tools' God gave them to destroy me.

"They shoved me into the adjoining room and threw me on the bed. They'd planned well. They tied lengths of rope to my wrists and ankles. While four of them held the bonds, flipping me this way and that, the fifth could rape me in any way he chose.

"Fortunately, I lost consciousness again and again. I don't know how many times they had me. When they'd exhausted their ability, the hawk-nosed man said, 'I suppose I'd better take the filthy bitch back and throw her in the carnival lot.'

"When he pulled on his suit, the others untied the ropes and threw my torn clothes on top of me. I struggled to gather them around me. I started to get to my feet when the youngest, who wasn't much older than you, Rog, shouted, 'Hey! Look guys! I win the prize! I got it up again. I'm gonna' have her one more time.'

"He slapped me to the bed. The others gathered quickly, their arms around each other's shoulders. As if cheering on the high school football team, they shouted drunkenly, 'Go, Brent, go! Go, Brent, go! Go, Brent, go!' He raped me to the rhythm of their voices."

Sharee closed her eyes and cried. We joined her.

I was overcome by shame. The devastating poetry of her narration had torn my soul. She'd told me I was a man. Men had done this to her.

I whispered softly, "Sharee, I'm leavin' the show. I'm the one who stands on the platform and invites men in to look at the three of you in a way that leads to this. I'm partly responsible for what happened to you."

She protested, "No, Rog. Don't leave. You're only doing your job."

I replied, "Then I've got to do some other kind of job."

I looked at her unimaginably battered body and choked out, "Before I go, I'm gonna' make you a promise, Sharee. I will never touch a woman outside of love and outside of marriage."

I've kept that promise to her across the years.

I made one final whispered request: "Sharee, can you forgive me?"

A twisted smile inched across her battered face as she replied, "Sometimes forgiveness needs to be gifted when the giver feels it's not really necessary. Sure, Rog, I forgive you, if you need it."

I tenderly kissed her cheek. I wished I could have touched half a strawberry to her lips.

After hugging each of the others, I left the trailer.

I returned to the tiger van. Old S'tooth was snoring in his cage. I quickly packed my few belongings in the battered cardboard liquor case.

As I opened the door, I sensed someone watching me. I turned. A shaft of moonlight illumined the agonized Jesus on the cross. He appeared particularly troubled. If he carried all the world's pain, he was torn by the rape of Sharee.

I reached up and stroked my index finger over his twisted face as I'd seen Ben do to so many people. At the moment, I was "faith blind." I hoped the touch would somehow keep me journeying across a landscape of hope.

I headed down the dusty country road under the cold stare of Venus, the morning star.

The Seashore

I typed the final sentence. Struggling to my feet, I stretched out the muscle fatigue which had built up over the long night's writing. My movement disturbed the cockroaches who rustled across the shack floor. I stepped carefully to the door, attempting to avoid squishing an omnipresent insect beneath my bare toes.

I walked out on the sand. Venus hung there in the sky as she had so many years ago. I looked back toward the shack. The old blue heron was huddled on the roof, focusing his endless meditation on the star.

I plunged into the cold waters of the sea. I swam hard. I would disappear beneath the surface for as long as breath would last. I was avoiding the harsh stare from the heart of the universe eternally reminding me of my guilt-laden role in the destruction of someone I loved so much. Her words of forgiveness had not registered in my soul's depths. They twisted around inside me along with the senseless but real guilt I felt for hating my daddy — the guilt for wishing him dead and then having him die.

I swam harder. There was no way on land or sea I could outrun or outswim the pursuing demons. I had to engage them.

On the shack roof I saw the beckoning figure of the old heron. The mist rising from the battered shingles reminded me of sacred smoke. I remembered the old shaman, Tony Great Turtle, greeting the dawn with a smudge of sage, sweet grass and juniper nestled in an abalone shell.

He always assured me that the only person who could really destroy me was myself. If I wrote the final story, perhaps I would discover peace which heals.

I slowly swam to shore. The heron floated down on the rising air currents of the morning. I knelt, dug out a handful of sand crabs and extended them to him as an offering.

I whispered, "Hang in there with me on this one, Tony, dear friend. I've never needed you more."

I walked slowly across the sand, allowing the brisk breeze to dry me. I stepped inside and went straight to the computer. I had to write away the pain.

I paused for a moment to look out toward the sea. The old heron was outlined in the cobwebbed window.

Something Like Forgiveness

It was the summer of my seventeenth year. During the week I was back working in Axel Torquelson's grocery store.

On Sundays I was making a name for myself doing supply preaching in little Methodist churches peppered across southern Minnesota and northern Iowa. I'd completed a course of study and was proudly in possession of a "local preacher's license."

I'd read about a never-to-be-forgotten minister named Henry Drummond, who'd traveled all over the country preaching just one sermon: "Acres of Diamonds." I thought that sounded like a good deal.

I knocked out a minor masterpiece called "The Necessity of Forgiveness."

It was much in demand. One day, a caller inquired, "Are you the same Roger Robbennolt that preached that wonderful sermon about forgiveness in Fairwater City? My cousin Bertie said it was just about the best thing she'd ever heard. She's been having problems with her husband, Tilman, and so she made him go a second time when you preached it in Traverse Junction. She figures if you preach it here in Bingham's Meadow she'll bring him again. Maybe he'll finally get the picture. The third time's a charm, you know."

The proffered date was open.

During my brief stint with the carnival we had performed in many of these same little towns. Nagging at the edge of my consciousness was the possibility that someone might recognize me in my former role as spieler in the carnival cooch show. Such identification might becloud their appreciation of my new role as purveyor of the Word of God.

I drove my borrowed car into a dusty church parking lot on a hot July Sunday.

Approaching the squat, stolid building, I noticed a disproportionately large cast-iron cross rising up from an uncompleted tower. The weathering of the bricks made it appear to have been uncompleted for about forty years. Budgetary concerns obviously ruled the day.

A woman in a wildly flowered dress wearing an enormous hat decorated with the same fabric swept down the long flight of steps leading to the sanctuary.

She effused, "I'm Pearl Pinklewood, and you must be that wonderful young preacher we've been hearing so much about, but you're real lucky to have met me first because I'm your lay reader for the morning and I'll do everything but preach, though the deacons said if they couldn't get you I might just have to share a few words, but before I take you in to see the sanctuary you've got to see the pride of Bingham's Meadow Methodist Church because so many people have worked real hard to realize Violet Rosewater's dream after she returned from her life-changing visit to the Holy Land where she had a vision that God wanted her to plant a Biblical Garden right here at Bingham's Meadow Methodist Church containing all the plants mentioned in the Scriptures that would grow in northern Iowa."

If she'd paused to take a breath during this excitable narration, I'd missed it. We rounded a corner of the building and were confronted by a neatly tended patch in which some odd little plants were struggling against the demons of summer heat and rocky soil.

Pearl continued, "We think it's wonderful, just wonderful, that Violet led us to do this before she died because every time I walk by here I feel just blessed because on her deathbed she left me in charge of the sanctification of the garden, and I feel closer to the Spirit every time I do the sprinkling, because you see she brought back a big bottle of water from the Jordan River, figuring that any water that flowed around Jesus at his baptism would insure the survival of the plants, but she also took a few drops a day herself thinking it might be good for her arthritis but she got this awful intestinal thing which dehydrated her so bad that she just faded away, and the Board of Trustees of the church and the Bingham's Meadow Town Council voted to suspend the rules and allow her to do her final resting right here in the garden, which I regret a little because every time I come out here I get all choked up just remembering that blessed little soul."

Pearl mercifully proceeded to do so. I was out of breath just listening to her. I spoke admiringly of the garden as we ascended a set of rickety back steps which led directly into the chancel of the church.

I was encouraged to try the pulpit. This was a challenge since it had been constructed for the man pastoring here when the church was built. He must have been a distant relative of my dwarf friend, Oscar Sidelka. I assured Pearl the pulpit would be fine since I had my sermon well-memorized after its numerous deliveries. I wouldn't need to see any notes.

She informed me that the usual pattern would be followed after the service. The senior deacon and his family would take me home for dinner before my return to Pheasant Valley. My hosts would be a little late for the service because they had to deliver a visiting distant cousin to the Greyhound Bus depot.

Folks began arriving. Pearl assured me that there'd be a big congregation because my fame had preceded me. She waved to an enormous woman dragging a dour-faced man down the aisle. Bertie and Tilman had arrived. I did recall meeting them in a couple of other settings.

The organist swung into the opening hymn, "I Walk in the Garden Alone." My mind wandered. I knew the hymn had been written to lift up the experience of Mary Magdalene on Easter morning. God had used a dancing woman of questionable reputation to open to the world the reality of resurrection. My thoughts strayed to Sharee.

Midway through the hymn the swinging doors at the rear of the sanctuary opened. A stunning, beautifully coifed woman entered and led two elegant children — a girl of seven and a boy of five — into the rear pew which the ushers had reserved for latecomers.

In a few moments the doors opened again. The family was joined by the hawk-nosed man in the gray flannel suit. His face was illuminated by light filtered through a stained glass window depicting a chastely-leafed Adam and Eve being banished from Eden while the snake, still upright, smirked in the background before being condemned to crawl on his belly.

As the man moved into the shadowed pew, his face mirrored that of my mindsick daddy. A wave of nausea hit me. I escaped through the side door. In the memorial garden containing all the plants of the Bible which would grow in northern Iowa, I lost the bountiful breakfast my mother always fortified me with before preaching. I was careful not to violate the final resting place of Violet Rosewater.

I stumbled back into the chancel. Pearl was reading the Old Testament lesson: Hosea 11: 1-9. She concluded with the words, "I will not execute the fierceness of mine anger, I will not return to destroy Ephraim: for I am God, and not man; the Holy One in the midst of thee: and I will not enter into the city."

The rest of the service is a blur in my mind. I must have preached my famous sermon about forgiveness. After Pearl's benediction I saw the reluctant Tilman scurrying for the door pursued by a determined Bertie. I was quickly surrounded by well-wishers.

In the distance I saw the hawk-nosed man followed by six deacons disappear into a back room. I wondered how many of them had participated in the desecration of Sharee.

The man's wife approached me, smiling warmly. The little boy grabbed my leg. Grinning up at me, he queried, "Will you read us stories when you come for dinner at my house? I really like you."

His mother chuckled and commented, "You preached a wonderful sermon. The children and I will walk on ahead and fry chicken. You ride to our house with my husband after his brief meeting to plan the Lord's Supper for next Sunday. I hope you won't find the children pests."

I muttered what must have been an incomprehensible response. She turned to leave. The children followed, waving good-bye. Other worshipers crowded around.

The sanctuary emptied except for Pearl who had fluttered effusively in the background as I was greeted. She extended a damp palm and did a breathless three-minute summary of my sermon and what she had enjoyed most and mostest and how glad she was that I was beginning so young and how proud she was of her son, Brent, who was just about my age and was now the youngest deacon in the history of the church and how she was so sorry to have to leave me because her husband Woodard was still in bed from his ruptured appendix and the attendant surgery, the details of which were run by me at breakneck speed.

At the mention of Brent's name I remembered that a kid named Brent had staged the final event in the gang rape of Sharee.

I boldly interrupted her verbal flow to assure her that I would keep her husband in my prayers. I turned to leave. She adjusted her great hat to a sun-defying angle and disappeared through the swinging doors.

I decided to slip out to my car and depart as quickly as possible. My plan was truncated by the appearance of the hawk-nosed man. The rest of his committee must have exited through a rear door. He moved quickly toward me, his hand extended, a flow of compliments preceding him. I faked a cough and covered my mouth with my right hand to avoid his touch.

As we stepped into the parking lot, I felt the nausea sweep over me again. I was confronted by the long gray Lincoln. He beckoned me to the passenger side. I wondered if there would be vestiges of Sharee's bloodstains on the cushions.

I stood rooted in place. He stared at me strangely as if struggling to relate my face to a familiar image from the past. He queried, "You look awful, young man. Is there anything I can do for you? You'd better get in the car out of the hot sun. I'll take you home, and you can lie down."

My feet recovered their powers of locomotion. I stalked him the way S'tooth used to move toward the audience before his climactic roar. My body was contorted by the rising gorge of anger.

I rasped out, "The only thing you could do for me would be to drop dead right here before my very eyes."

A wave of recognition flowed over his face as I whispered, "You destructive bastard. I know what you and your buddies did to one of the dearest people in my life: Sharee, the lead dancer in Blind Ben See's Carnival of Wonders."

He blanched and reached to support himself. His hand encountered the aerial which snapped off through the force of his dead weight. He grabbed the rearview mirror and steadied himself as he staggered from my revelation.

I crouched before him, ready to spring. My eyes burned into his. He began to babble disconnected phrases: "I was dared . . . my manhood questioned by my drinking buddies . . . we were all drunk at the time . . . have spent hours on my knees begging God's forgiveness . . . wife and I not getting along at the time . . . none of us in very happy marriages . . . took out all our anger at every woman in the world on the carnival dancer . . . she was our scapegoat and we took her to the wilderness . . . please forgive me . . . please forgive us . . . we raped her again and again without any real satisfaction . . . without any real pleasure . . . when I went back to the cabin after dumping her in the carnival lot there wasn't any triumph . . . please forgive me . . . if you ever see her again ask her forgiveness . . . you preached a powerful sermon on forgiveness . . . please forgive me . . . ."

He was sobbing.

I snapped. My right foot shot out, finding the soft center of his groin. He screamed and doubled up. In fast succession my left foot shot two blows to his kneecaps. He collapsed in the parking lot gravel, his arms embracing the right front tire.

Every word of profanity I'd learned under the tutelage of my father whipped through high noon heat as I kicked him again and again. I was sobbing as I assured him that I was going to kick him as many times as he and his cohorts had entered Sharee.

I could not stop the return of those images of that night of terror when my mindsick daddy raped me. In the shadow of the auto their faces were one.

He went limp.

I staggered across the parking lot toward my borrowed auto. I'd taken vengeance for myself and Sharee.

As I neared my car, I was stopped by a distinct voice from the center of my heart. It was Sharee reciting those lines from W. H. Auden's "Songs and Other Musical Pieces":

O stand, stand at the window
As the tears scald and start;
You must love your crooked neighbor
With your crooked heart.

I paused, my anger shattered by that celestial, saving voice. I hesitated for a moment, then turned and stumbled across the gravel. I was totally broken. I also felt in the depths of my being that I might be headed toward wholeness.

I knelt in the dust of the church parking lot. The wrought iron cross cast a long shadow over us in the intense sunlight of high noon. I gathered both the battered man and my mindsick daddy in my arms.

The Seashore

I was beyond tears. I felt overwhelmingly empty and overwhelmingly full. I also felt some guilt. I'd lived through a rare experience of insight. I'd let it get away from me. I'd let the old anger shred my psyche without tuning in on a regular basis to the healing which had begun adjacent to the biblical garden.

I looked up at the crucifix. Christ triumphant was smiling. I took down my worn one-eyed bear and cuddled him for a long, long time. He'd always been a sustaining presence. He'd been there through most of the stories of my life. Maybe if I held him long enough this time, the healing would hang in my heart of hearts.

The old heron broke my reverie with the familiar tap of his beak on the window. It was three o'clock in the afternoon. Pausing to set the computer on "print," I stepped out on the deserted beach. Tony preceded me to the shore. He bowed his head toward the unusually placid water. I was reminded of a line from an old hymn: "Holy, holy, holy! All the saints adore thee, casting down their golden crowns beside the glassy sea."

The sky was intensely blue. The rays of the lowering sun seemed to penetrate my naked body. Every taut nerve let go. I slipped into the quiet ocean. The old heron waded out beside me. Lowering a great wing into the Gulf, he swept a gentle cascade of water over my head. I was a child again standing in Lake Sumac, the holy lake, with Tony Great Turtle, the old Lakota shaman, pouring a stream of symbolic healing over my shivering body. I knew I was being washed whiter than snow.

I lazed in the gentle rocking of the surf. I let the anger within me flow out. I knew I would never release it all. I'd have some bad moments. For now, I would simply let the waves carve it down to a manageable size like a sand sculpture.

I was jolted into the moment by the antics of the heron. He would fly a ways up the beach, circle back and then realight over the roof of the shack. Time must be passing quickly, I thought. I had some sharing to do.

I pulled myself out of the water, ran across the intervening sand, pulled on my Speedo, ragged cutoffs and golden shirt, tore off the final two tales from the computer printout and plodded up the tire marks in the sand toward the golden throne.

As I walked up the beach, I was aware of a splash of brilliant red moving up and down near Blind Ben's chair. Coming nearer, I realized it was Ramblin' Rose.

She was wearing a scarlet satin dress. Her raven hair was piled high upon her head. Golden sandals graced her feet. A crystal necklace obscured the scar on her throat. The solemn expanse of Ben's preacherly coat was enlivened by a fresh red carnation in the lapel. A basket sat at the side of the fading chair.

I exploded in amazement: "What gives with you two?"

Blind Ben See explained, "Rose decided a celebration would be in order when you finished the nine tales. She thought we ought to dress for it."

Rose inquired, "How do I look, kid?"

I assured her, "You can dance in my cooch show any day."

Her laughter rose to join the lively chatter of gulls circling overhead.

Ben slowly knelt down and opened the basket, explaining, "Rose thinks celebrating the success of a soon-to-be-famous author should involve refreshments. Spread out the buffalo hide, and we'll begin our feast. We might all be better able to handle the last two stories with a bit of fortification."

He set out a bottle of champagne, three antique Coca Cola glasses and a box of Ritz crackers.

Rose said, "There's even some napkins in the bottom. I've

bin clearin' stuff out and throwin' stuff away. Ben and me are sortin' down to bare minimums — sorta' gettin' our lives tidied up. I was about to put my napkin collection in the trash burner. Every town we played, I'd go to the most frequented eatery, order coffee and pick up a few of their napkins. I happened to run across some from the Dew Drop Inn in Pheasant Valley. I thought they might be especially appropriate."

I hugged her for her thoughtfulness.

I was given the honor of popping the cork. It rose through the rays of the setting sun and settled on the salt waves. Two gulls squabbled over it.

I filled the glasses. Ben proposed a toast: "To you, Rog. May you always be a spieler of the Sacred."

We sipped and nibbled. Rose finally said, "It's time to hear the last tales, Rog. I think yer capable of reading and drinking at the same time."

I warned them, "I may have a rough time reading these aloud. They touch the deepest part of me."

Ben interjected, "All stories should do that."

I continued, "I'm going to read them both without stopping since they're a pair."

Ben took Rose in the crook of his right arm. They settled back against the chair.

I read the tales.

When I finished, Ben reached out his left arm. I snuggled against him. Rose reached for my hand. We were in perfect touch.

Ben finally spoke, almost inaudibly: "Curious, ain't it — how folks come together? If Sharee hadn't been desecrated, you would have never found this vessel of writing in which to sail toward saving forgiveness. You were a bit like that champagne cork floating aimlessly on the waves. I guess what this life really boils down to is the decisions we make in response to what happens to us — what we do with what comes our way.

"I let lust destroy the first half of my life. I bought the carnival. I felt useful again giving folks a place of refuge in a lot of different ways. The Scartown family became what I always wanted my church to be: a place where the sacred could never be destroyed inside a person — where there was always somebody to love you back toward meaning again."

I assured him, "Ben, that's what you and Rose are to me — folks who loved me back to meaning when I was a carnival kid. Now, when I was groping for words to heal the hatred which was consuming me, you appear on a deserted beach and save me once again by listening."

Rose stopped me: "Okay, so we've had some kind of a minor miracle on a gravel beach off Gibtown. Let's not beat it into the ground with our philosophizing. Just let it be and celebrate it with a final glass of bubbly and a handful of crackers. I suppose yuh'll leave tomorrow, Rog, having finished yer masterpiece. That makes this kind of a last supper."

We shared the remaining elements in silence.

As she gathered up the remains of our feast, Rose reminded me, "By the way, Rog, Mario's cross was on loan. Now that yer about to rejoin the world, I'd kinda' like to have it back."

I responded, "I'm going to spend all day reading over what I've written and packing up my few belongings. That moon will be full tomorrow night. Since I won't have new tales to tell, why don't we gather about nine o'clock and see what kind of magic it might work on us. I'll bring the cross with me."

There was a long pause. Ben reached up and traced the landscape of my face — then Rose's. He responded quietly, "That'd be just fine."

I hugged them goodnight. They seemed reluctant to let me go.

I hiked down the beach. Far out to sea I saw the heron flying parallel to me.

It seemed strange to walk into the shack with no images crying out to be written. I collapsed on the cot. I'd not slept for twenty-four hours. I fell into an unhaunted, sacramental sleep.

I awakened at noon the next day feeling a kind of spiritual release I'd never known before. I ran for the water and plunged in. For the first time in my life I felt really clean. I floated on my back and whistled calliope tunes. Above me, the looping flight of the heron mirrored my merriment.

I spent the afternoon hiking to the store, retrieving my car and packing up the unread books. Early in the evening I pulled on my cutoffs and golden shirt, gently removed the cross from its spike and headed out for the two-mile hike up the beach. I kept having to move a bit inland to avoid soaking my shorts in the unusually high tide and steady surf. The heron was nowhere to be seen.

As I neared the golden throne, Blind Ben and Ramblin' Rose were nowhere in sight. I was early. Though the sky was beginning to gild in the east, the great moon had not appeared.

When I was twenty or thirty yards away from the peeling chair, I was distracted by a flash of red in its seat. I picked up my pace.

Arriving, I was confronted by a curious sight. In the seat of Ben's command post lay his clothes neatly folded: his preacherly suit, boxer shorts, socks and, on top, the golden shirt. Over them all was Rose's red silk dress with her underwear folded chastely inside.

Their shoes nestled together on the sand. Bare footprints led to what an hour before had been the water's edge.

I quickly scanned the sea. There was no sign of anyone. I called their names. My voice echoed back to me unanswered.

I put the crucifix atop their belongings, stripped and hit the water. Every few yards I paused and called their names, to no avail.

I began to tire. I flipped on my back. The great bloated moon rose bloodred over the eastern horizon. I was overcome by fear for the fate of Ben and Rose counterbalanced by an incredible sense of peace, which, for a moment, sang a siren's song to me. It would have been so easy to simply float into oblivion — easier than a rope in an attic.

Fortunately, Sharee's saving lines echoed once more. I still had a lot of love to give — and receive. My heart still had its crooked corners, but my sense of the Sacred alive in me was gloriously intact.

I swam slowly back to shore. I leaned against the chair. The eye on Ben's golden shirt was closed. I watched the moon pale as it struggled toward the zenith. It cast a golden highway across the gentle water.

I picked up the cross and waded into the moonlit path following the receding tide. I gently floated the carved wood, crucifixion-side up, on the gentle surf. One who had suffered so much might embrace the pain of the world and carry it into the wilderness of water.

An oblique rogue wave hit the cross and flipped it over. The smiling Christ triumphant floated into the distance, holding in his open arms Ramblin' Rose, Blind Ben See, a universe of stars — and me.

Between the saving figure and the Big Dipper flew the old heron.